THE STRANGER

⚜ CLUNY CLASSICS ⚜

RICCARDO BACCHELLI
The Mill on the Po: God Save You (BOOK ONE)
The Mill on the Po: Misery (BOOK TWO)
The Mill on the Po: Nothing New Under the Sun (BOOK THREE)

ROBERT HUGH BENSON
Come Rack, Come Rope
Dawn of All
The Light Invisible
None Other Gods

GEORGES BERNANOS
A Bad Dream
A Crime
Joy
Under the Sun of Satan

ORESTES BROWNSON
Like a Roaring Lion

MALACHY G. CARROLL
The Stranger

G. K. CHESTERTON
Wanderings over the World

MYLES CONNOLLY
The Bump on Brannigan's Head
Dan England and the Noonday Devil
Mr. Blue
The Reason for Ann & Other Stories
Three Who Ventured

ALICE CURTAYNE
House of Cards

GERTRUD VON LE FORT
The Pope from the Ghetto
The Veil of Veronica

JOSÉ MARÍA GIRONELLA
The Cypresses Believe in God (VOLUME ONE)
The Cypresses Believe in God (VOLUME TWO)

RUMER GODDEN
A Breath of Air
Five for Sorrow, Ten for Joy
In This House of Brede

CAROLINE GORDON
The Life and Passion of Aleck Maury
The Malefactors

NATHANIEL HAWTHORNE
The Shattered Fountain: Selected Tales

ELISABETH LANGGÄSSER
The Quest

FRANÇOIS MAURIAC
The Dark Angels
The Desert of Love
Genetrix
A Kiss for the Leper
The Lamb
The River of Fire
The Unknown Sea
Vipers' Tangle
What Was Lost

DOROTHY L. SAYERS
Whose Body?

IGNAZIO SILONE
Fontamara
Bread and Wine
The Seed Beneath the Snow

SIGRID UNDSET
The Burning Bush
The Wild Orchid
Four Stories
Images in a Mirror
Madame Dorthea

LEO L. WARD
Men in the Field: Eighteen Short Stories

THE STRANGER

A Novel

Malachy G. Carroll

CLUNY

Providence, Rhode Island

Cluny Media edition, 2018

For more information regarding this title
or any other Cluny Media publication,
please write to info@clunymedia.com, or to
Cluny Media, P.O. Box 1664, Providence, RI, 02901

ISBN: 978-1949899573

Cover design by Clarke & Clarke
Cover image: Claude Monet, *Still Life with Chrysanthemums*,
detail, 1878, oil on canvas
Courtesy of Wikimedia Commons

Contents

For my wife, Maureen, *on our first anniversary*

CHAPTER THE FIRST

A mill, standing in from the road, made him pause. The gray of his suit was whitened with dust, but it was a well-tailored suit, and you knew at a glance that its owner could wear it. When you looked at him, you noticed the face most of all: a face of character, a face that showed reserves of strength, a cultured face, penciled by some secret sorrow in lines that were firm but not hard. They softened now as he looked at the mill, and a certain wistfulness came into his face, like that with which a person looks at a sleeping child, or a man thinks of the time when the dew was on his dreams. Then, for a moment, a little smile played about his lips and the firm lines softened.

There was joy in the morning: in the hedgerows sprinkled with water pearls; in the first, fine, careless rapture of a blackbird, singing his song thrice over; in the breeze passing over the wheat, like fingers caressing plush against the pile. Even the little village looked warm and comforting. Its houses seemed to gather cozily in the sun, like cozy grandmothers exchanging cozy little bits of gossip. Among

1

them was the public house of Mrs. McGough: a solid house, four-square, comfortable, eminently sensible—in fact, the goodly qualities of Mrs. McGough herself told in stone. It had, too, that little touch of careless grace, so necessary to true elegance. The solid G of S. McGough—set in solid relief above the window—had slipped half its moorings, and leaned tipsily on the C. It was like Mrs. McGough there, too; for Mrs. McGough, always neat, always presentable at all times, wore the strings of her apron dangling ungracefully about her knees. When you looked at the strings, you thought of the tipsy G; when you saw the tipsy G, you thought of the strings. They were both touches of the careless meant to underline the perfection of the rest, and I think the neighbors would have found something amiss had Mrs. McGough remoored that G, or tied those apron strings. Things in the village would, somehow, never have seemed the same.

When Mrs. McGough said she just looked at a man, and didn't "put much heed in him," she meant that she merely noticed that he was stiff and stout and going bald; that he had protruding eyes, big ears, and a mole over his right eye; that tie, suit, and shoes were a dissonance. So, when Mrs. McGough said she "didn't take a good look at him," you suspected that perhaps his most secret sins remained undetected.

The door opened, with that hesitancy and that pause in which there is already a kind of implicit apology. She looked up from her pewter polishing and glanced casually at the Stranger. Not a giant, but firm and well made; dust coating his shoes and the bottoms of his trousers; a cultured face, shadowed but not embittered. That quick glance of Mrs. McGough was like a penny placed in one of those slot machines which give you a description of the man you are. She registered—a gentleman with a load on his mind.

"Good morning," he said. "Isn't it a lovely morning?"

"Aye, surely," she answered. "A glorious morning. And what can I do for you?"

She had noticed that there was something English about the way he spoke—but it wasn't that kind of accent which Mary Ryan brought home with her, when she stayed overnight in the Isle of Man. It was that loveliest of spoken English—an Irish accent whose consonants have been shaped by long shoulder-rubbing with English speech, but which has retained its softness and the purity of the vowels.

"Could I have some biscuits and lemonade, please?" he asked.

Yes, the voice was just as she had expected—a mellow cultured voice. She always referred to a voice like his in terms of color, as a "brown" voice, for she had a rather disconcerting habit of thinking in color. Nobody knew what exactly she meant by a "brown" voice, but they knew it as the crowning grace of a gentleman for Mrs. McGough. ("I thought she was a lady at first," she said to her husband about a newcomer to the village, "and then she started talking in a red voice.") So Mrs. McGough nodded her head in sage self-approval, as she bent behind the counter to get some lemonade. She liked to find the voice confirming the first impression. A gentleman. Then she straightened, and placed the purchases on the counter.

"That will be tenpence, please," she said.

The hand came to her with the money, and for a second she looked at it with a kind of shock. It was a rough hand, hardened and calloused by laboring work. The hand of an Esau and the voice of a Jacob. Mrs. McGough was suddenly very puzzled indeed.

"Newry fair busy?" she asked.

"Yes, it was," he answered, somewhat taken aback. "It was a good enough fair."

Little of his mind on the fair, Mrs. McGough registered.

"Well, I hope that man o' mine does well at it," she continued, "for he's away with some sleek heifers that should look like the kine o' Bashan, beside yon skinny beasts from around Clogoghue."

The Stranger's eyes lit up with surprised appreciation, very flattering to her. She could talk well, and was the kind of person who could not join a society without suddenly finding herself president of it. His face thawed in a lovely half smile, and in the few minutes she spoke with him, she watched that smile come and go, like sunshine chasing shadow. Yet, as she turned to go into the kitchen, she knew very well that the smile was but the swift glance of light on the surface of the shadow, the shadow always returning. That face mystified her, but she dismissed it as a schoolboy does an unsolved "x," and got down to the practicalities of a husband's dinner. It is an essential of a good businesswoman that she should eschew immediately all thoughts beyond the reaches of her soul—because there's no money in them.

Ten minutes later, when the good woman had reached a critical moment in the simultaneous supervision of four pots, and had completely forgotten her customer, there was a small, rather apologetic knock on the counter.

"Good luck to them," she muttered. "What a time they take to come. Go and see who it is, Nell. My hands are greasy."

Nell rose from her potato-peeling, dried her hands, and went into the shop. In half a minute, she was back.

"Mam, do you know anyone in the village who would take a lodger?"

"And in the name of all that's wonderful, who wants to stay in this backwash?"

"The stranger out in the shop."

Mrs. McGough squinted four pots out of focus and refocused the man she had just served, for she had completely forgotten him.

"Keep an eye to yon pots," she said, "and I'll go out myself."

"You were asking about lodgings?" she said, as she came into the shop.

"Yes," he answered. "Perhaps you know someone, or maybe you have a room here?"

Mrs. McGough studied him in silence for a long fifteen seconds. There was a sharp look in her eye which would have given you some idea of the Particular Judgment, for she was now looking at him with all the shrewdness of an Irish peasant-cum-businesswoman, and you would have felt that what wasn't "naked and open" to her eye, in that fifteen seconds, didn't matter a lot. When she spoke, it was not a simple answer, but a judgment delivered.

"We don't usually keep lodgers, but right enough, we have a room, and I don't know any other house in the village that has. Anyhow, come and have a look at it."

The room was one of those little ones that are tucked away at the back of the house and pink-washed for compensation. There was a faded carpet on the floor, an iron bedstead, a washstand with the usual floral etceteras, a small table, a frail chair also pink, and an armchair with the usual nostalgic look of faded gentility. A large gaudy oleograph of the Sacred Heart simpered in the corner, and a small statue of St. Anthony simpered at a simpering Child.

In fact, as Mrs. McGough might have said, the whole mood of the room was decidedly "pink."

"There," she said, as they stood on the threshold. "Does that like you?"

His eyes were on the little window and on the peace of the view and on the peace it all promised.

"Yes, thank you," he said. "This will be fine."

They stood in silence for a moment.

"My name is Murray," he went on.

Mrs. McGough waited. She seldom asked personal questions, chiefly because she believed an Irishman will give one his whole history anyhow, if one only waits.

His next remark shot off at a tangent and somewhat disconcerted her.

"Do you think, Mrs. McGough, that there is any chance of work around here?"

"Well, that depends; and if you ask me on what, I'll say that again depends," she answered enigmatically.

It reminded him of how he had once, as a child, watched a monkey in the zoo swinging from another monkey, and a third swinging from it.

"What sort of work would you like?" she added, for when she looked at him she thought of books and ledgers and pens and blotters, but his hands puzzled her.

"It's all one to me, for I've taken a turn at most kinds."

"Doesn't sound as if you made much of a success of any, Mr. Murray," she said, with a shrewd side glance at him.

For a second, she surprised a look of pain in his face, as though her remark had gone home. However, it was with a smile that he answered slowly:

"Yes, I believe that you are right."

By this time they had descended the stairs and were in the kitchen. Her husband had come in.

"This is a Mr. Murray, Jimmy. I'm letting him have the back room."

"How are you," Jimmy said, "and what fancy did you take to our big city?"

"Well, I've been something of a rolling stone," Murray said, "and I thought it might be no harm to stand for a while and gather some moss. I like it here. It's quiet."

7

"Faith and it's all that. Gets up and shakes itself once a month for a big fair, that's three quarters of its movement."

"And the other quarter," Mrs. McGough put in, "is more or less from pub to pub of our nine pubs. But the gentleman was asking about work in the neighborhood. Any kind of work."

Jimmy thought for a while. His pipe gurgled in its twisted shank as though it were whispering advice.

"I wonder," he said turning to his wife, "if Patch Rafferty got back his job in McCourt's mill?"

"Not unless McCourt is a bigger fool than many a one locked up," she answered. "Patch Rafferty," she explained to her visitor, "is one of them sponges dipped in a barrel of Guinness and put going on two rickety legs. McCourt discovered last week what half the parish knew last year—that Patch Rafferty was pocketing half the profits from the mill. The business was going down anyhow, for Patch is a failure as a miller. A scourge and a scab, that's what he is."

"Well, in that case, I'd see McCourt before someone else does," Jimmy added.

"I'll go right now about it," said the Stranger, rising to go.

CHAPTER THE SECOND

"Wait a minute," McCourt called after him.

The man at the gate turned quietly and came back.

"You know, I am sorry to turn you away like this. But you have no papers, and you'll have heard that I have already been stung. Maybe you could get some papers in a few days, eh?"

"I'm sorry," came the quiet answer. "I can get no papers. And please don't apologize for refusing to take me on. It was foolish of me to think you would."

Something in the quality of the man's voice made McCourt pause.

"Now, look here, maybe there's someone in the village...."

"No, not even that," came the answer, and the man turned away saying: "Well, I'm sorry to have troubled you."

It is a hard thing to see the ebb of hope in a man's eyes, and McCourt saw it now. He watched him go and bit his lip in sudden indecision. He had never heard Pascal's maxim about the heart's reasons of which the head knows nothing, but he acted on one of them now.

"All right, I'll take you," he said.

There was a deep, quiet joy on the Stranger's face as he thanked him. They spoke for some time together. His father had been a miller in Kerry many years ago, he told McCourt, and he had worked with him. He had done no work like that since, but one doesn't forget these things. McCourt talked of some new machinery in the mill, and suggested that they should go and look at it. They walked across the field toward the mill. As they did so, two sullen eyes under a mop of red hair watched them through a gap in the hedge. The face that went with those eyes was a hollow, bony one that blended the stupidity of the cow with the cunning of the fox. A stiff stubble of several days' growth, covering lips and chin, added a grotesque touch of the hedgehog. Cow, fox, and hedgehog would indeed have summed the man. Hostile and suspicious, the eyes followed every movement of the two men until the door of the mill hid them. In a very short time, the noise of machinery was heard, at first with an uncertainty and hesitation in the sound, as of a man feeling his way; then with an increasing sense of confidence, as though dormant skill was coming alive again in the worker's hands. As the first staccato sounds stabbed the quiet of the darkening fields, a cynical leer twisted the mouth of the redheaded listener. A dud, he said. But as the sound steadied its rhythm, a dull angry red surged in the scraggy neck, suffused the face, and seemed to ebb into the fiery hair. A passing farmer had pulled up his cart near him, amazed at hearing the sound of the mill. He muttered to himself: "Well, if McCourt has *him* back, he's the biggest eejit out!" Then he spotted the red head like an exotic bloom in the hedge, and he whipped up his horse very quickly indeed. Everyone knew Patch Rafferty, his temper and treachery.

Patch had been McCourt's miller for several years— with great profit to Patch. All the intelligence he possessed was harnessed to the task of lining his pockets at the expense of his employer, of his customers, of the quality of his flour.

But this lining had a trick of becoming the lining of some publican's pockets, so that at any given moment, Patch could be found living on the milled edge of his shilling. The fire of life that McCourt tended had so many irons in it that he could attend to some of them only and had to depend on others to care for the rest. It was easy, therefore, for a man like Patch so to poke the fire with one of those irons that most of the heat came his way. In a sense, Patch's tragedy was that he was wasting his time. He had all the qualities required to make good in the Ireland of World War II and the first years of an exhausted peace, for the border bubbled at his feet, a potential river of gold. He should have discovered that his talents had fitted him to cross the border and rise to the ranks of the new aristocracy there—the aristocracy of the black market. Instead of slouching in a hedge, as he was doing now, he could long since have bought a house that had been made beautiful with centuries of quiet culture, have lounged collarless over the gate, and demonstrated with an unanswerable spit that the Island of Saints and Scholars had finally come of age as the Island of Saints, a few Scholars, and a swarm of highly respected Swindlers. Instead of being a man with reputation lost for a few shillings, he could be wearing the shining halo of the new third order of the S's, the halo of the "smart boyo."

The two men had emerged from the mill and appeared to be chatting amicably. They crossed the field just out of earshot, and parted at the gate. The Stranger came along the road toward him. Patch glared at him as he passed, and saw a puzzled expression in the answering look. When he had gone past, Patch took a few steps forward with his fists clenched, hesitated, turned on his heel with a curse, and went off in the opposite direction. The moon had risen and was filling the countryside with the ghost of daylight.

At the corner of the road, a bicycle drew in beside the Stranger and a girl alighted, with a bright greeting, to walk beside him. He recognized her as Nell, the daughter of the McGough household. Nell was typical of the Irish market-town girl, fresh complexioned, dark, unconscious of the beauty of her laughing lips and the kindly blue of her eyes; but unconscious too, of the piety and passion that blended in every line of her, yet with every evidence that the piety ruled the passion. At the moment, Blessed Martin de Porres saw to that. She was returning from the Confraternity meeting which prayed weekly to him whom they called "the little black saint"—though he was not yet a saint nor was he so very little nor so very black either. But we like to make everything little, for then it awakens the Celtic mist-that-does-be-on-the-bog softness in us, or so the Americans think anyhow; we rather like black—the priest's color and the color of the moods in our music—and as to the saint part of it, sure we all know he's in heaven anyhow. Nell was quite eloquent about him. Wasn't it wonderful, now, the way he could get the rats to obey him, and the way he put a cat and a mouse eating from the same dish? And there was more to it than far-off things, for didn't Kitty Kelly hear the vet himself saying the calf would die in an hour, and look at it now? Old Ma O'Hare's little granddaughter is up and about now, and she supposed to be doomed to the bed for years if you could believe the doctors.

"Somehow, when I think of him," she laughed, looking up at the sky, "I see his little black face shining in all the vast whiteness of heaven, like our Peter's when he's playing in the back and the sheets are on the line. And there's a great kindness in it."

"But surely," he said, smiling quietly, "we have saints of our own we can turn to. Isn't there St. Brigid now," he went on, slipping into the poetry of her mood, "who looks down on us with all the morning freshness of Irish Christianity brimming her lovely eyes? Wouldn't she speak for you?"

"Now, wouldn't you think yourself and old Father Sheridan were in league," she countered, laughing gaily. "He said one day that the whiteness of Brigid was still in the lovely quiet of Faughart, if we only had eyes to see it. But we have eyes only for foreigners, he said, for St. Anthony and St. Philomena, and now, Blessed Martin de Porres. You should have heard him joking after the Legion meeting last week...

'Didn't St. Brendan sail away looking for a new world and do you think he couldn't find your thimble as well as any foreigner? And isn't St. Brigid a lovely virgin too? And as for Blessed Martin—do you know, he'll start a row in heaven yet, for I hear he found Mrs. O'Neill's purse for her, and St. Anthony has filed a complaint with the Angel Gabriel about it. That's what the rumbling in heaven was last week—it wasn't thunder at all, it was St. Anthony tramping up and down the floor of heaven, letting off steam.' But sure everyone knows Father Sheridan and his jokes. I'm sure the saints tell each other his latest about them. It's one of the ways he has of hiding his own holiness even from himself. For we all know he's a saint himself."

They were now passing Father Sheridan's house, and she pointed it out to him. Moonlight and a milky haze lay on the fruit trees of the little orchard, and the stone statue of St. Brigid crowning the entrance was more lovely for a dimness of outline that softened it into flesh. At her feet, in glimpses of silver, the newly sprayed vegetables showed like a carpet laid for her wandering feet. In the shadows of the little drive stood a rugged miniature of that splendid monument of pagan Ireland, the stone of Proleek. When you came to know Father Sheridan—the nobly chiseled head, the thick drooping eyebrows that seemed to thatch the blue eyes—you thought of that stone standing in the cleansing shadow of the Christian cross; you thought of Brigid, clothed in the beauty of the moonlight, keeping watch. For these were the symbols of the deeper things in a man who might have been an old

Druid in the morning of Christianity, fresh from Patrick's baptism, with light upon him from Brigid's eyes. The fancy would have arisen from an attempt to express the essential mellowness of the man and the splendidly Irish qualities of the priesthood in him. You felt the moonlight about you as the radiance of Brigid, and you thought of the priest whose life was made lovely by his love for her loveliness, the priest who prayed the mantle of Brigid as the spiritual sky of his parish, shadowing every soul. But there was nothing aloof in all this, for the sympathy of the man had caused him to dip his consecrated hands deep in the rich, warm suds of human life, that the tremor of God might be felt through human things. It was all this, sensed rather than exactly known that made the parishioners say he was "a grand priest."

For indeed, the deep piety of the man was something carefully hidden, to be sought behind the full, hearty laugh, or sensed with a surge of new courage, in the steady grip of his handshake. Yet, the commandments, the precepts, the counsels, and half the mysticism of Christianity were in the robustness of the man, blended with what Yeats called the "sanctity of the intellect." There is a type of sanctity whose face has so much of the angelic and so little of the human in it that it suggests the dry, precise lines of a diamond on glass. There is also a type, so rich with human feeling that it might best be drawn in charcoal, for charcoal makes a soft, dusty line that suggests a sympathy with human nature— poor, dusty, bat-eyed thing, that can keep its eyes lifted to the light only with grace and through pain. That you thought of showing his sanctity in lines which looked like little trails of dust would have pleased Father Seumas Sheridan very much indeed, for he would have claimed the dust as appropriate and laughed at the idea of your seeing any glimmerings of the angel in it. Indeed, it was very hard really to catch these glimmerings, for if there was one thing about which this most candid of men was crafty, it was in seeking every means of appearing very ordinary.

Had Nell and the Stranger turned in to visit him that night, they would have found him, breviary in hand, haunch-levering himself into a more comfortable position in his easy chair. They would have heard a ping from Beelzebub, the front spring, and a grunt from Flibbertigibbet, the back spring, as the springs sank rustily on their heels to give a little, grudging comfort to the old priest. For that old chair seemed a very nest of demons, and Father Sheridan loved it and them. "Well, you see," he would say, as, with a slow smile, he pointed to each of the unruly springs, "there's Beelzebub and there's Mephistopheles and there's Flibbertigibbet, three old devils forced to serve the Lord. If I doze over the breviary and fall to the right, old Beelzebub comes up with a ping and lands me one. And if I fall to the left, old Mephy and Flibby ping, wham, slam together." And he would lean down and pat each of them with mock affection.

But Nell and the Stranger did not turn in to see the old priest, though Nell suggested it, for the Stranger not only seemed disinclined to do so, but showed a certain fear. Nell knew the wise old Gaelic proverb that warns us to be neither well got nor ill got with the clergy, and she attributed his reluctance to this. There was a tremendous courtesy in the way he listened and spoke to her—a courtesy that flattered her and to which she was not very accustomed. Her fiancé, John Boyd, was very nice and very attentive, but she could not help noticing that there was more grace in a passing gesture of the Stranger than in all John's efforts at being gracious. Before they reached her house, she had already gained a great respect for him. A meal was ready for them, and they sat down to it with a will, for there was a sauce to hunger in the night air. The Stranger had little to say, but father, mother, and daughter glowed in the fine courtesy with which he listened. When they had eaten, the Stranger said he would take another stroll, and went out.

Nell sat looking into the fire. He had spoken pleasantly to her and to the family, he had laughed and joked, but she sensed a sadness behind it all. When the conversation had veered toward his own affairs, other than that of his coming employment in the mill, he had quickly directed it into a different channel. There was mystery about this man, and it was a mystery of sadness. She had watched him and listened to him carefully during the meal, and had found herself remembering a picture she had seen recently in a big art book at the local library. A face, with eyes that were troubled, yet strangely peaceful, looked at you, but behind that face the artist had painted a bleak landscape of marsh and mud. She thought of that picture as she listened to him, and she saw in it the symbol of the man: smiling eyes with shadows in the smile, a hint of sorrow and of torn things behind the laugh and the jest. She felt that he was keeping his mind on the company and on what was being said, only with an effort. There were brief moments of vagueness in the eyes— brief because checked by a vigilant courtesy—in which she thought she saw the shadow welling forward. She imagined that now, walking alone in the moonlight, where he had no call on his attention or his courtesy, he had become as a man who gropes in his own mist of loneliness, a shadowed man....

It was quiet in the kitchen now, with her mother out visiting the Wards and her father asleep on the old, horsehair sofa. She stood pensively looking into the garden, with the moon on her face. It was so peaceful she could not endure the thought of any sorrow, for sorrow was something foreign to flowers and soft moonlight and the song of a bird singing because he thought it was day. Yet, walking somewhere beyond those walls, was a man who carried into all that beauty the secret of a shadowy sorrow. Nell wished that in some strange way her sympathy could go out to him to warm the cold and desolate places in which, she felt, he secretly lived.

Impulsively, she turned from the window, reached up into her workbasket, and, scissors in hand, went into the garden. She went from bed to bed, selecting and cutting the flowers with great care. Now and then, she held them up to the light, looked at them, arranged them. The dew was on them and they lay cool on her arm. She bent her face to them, inhaling their perfume.

Returned to the house, she slipped quietly past her father. It would not do if the sound of running water in the scullery wakened him—there would be questions—so she tilted the big colored vase and let the water run down its side. Quickly she arranged her flowers and went toward the stairs. A big coal lump broke on the fire, and the dancing flames silhouetted her and her flowers on the wall. A moment later, she had put the vase of flowers in the little pink room—the Stranger's room.

He seemed the sort of man who would love flowers, she thought as, returned to the kitchen, she pulled up her chair to the fire. Still, it was a strange thing to do. What had come over her? It was simply that she was sorry for him. That he seemed to be lonely. But Nell was too emphatic about her feelings, and she remained somewhat bewildered. In spite of herself, she felt a blush mounting her neck and burning in her cheeks. She buried her face in her hands, and told herself not to be silly. Then she took down a photo of her fiancé that stood on the mantelpiece. She held it in the firelight and looked at it. Then, with a sigh, she replaced it.

Half a mile away, the moonlight lay on something much whiter than itself. In McCourt's kitchen, a few, handfuls of flour made a little cone on the table. McCourt lifted it and let it run through his fingers. It ran smoothly, and if they measured time in heaven, it looked not unworthy an angelic hourglass. It cascaded on the table in a white stream and rose again in a little mist that was like the ghost of its whiteness.

McCourt's intuition had been a good one.

CHAPTER THE THIRD

In the palmy days of Irish-Americanism, we heard much about "the voice of Erin"—an idea that could be rationalized from the songs of our Lady Blessington, Irish bard, as a tear, a smile in a dewy eye, bunches of Trinity-clarifying shamrock, and harps that twanged a tale of round towers, bearded poets, and banquet hall deserted. Queenly Banba stands up with a green twilight about her, clothed with the beauty of her fields. She is fair and there is no spot in her. But those of us for whom she is a daily reality, and not merely a nostalgic mirage of Atlantic greenness, have heard her voice broken by a cough—a dry, choking, ghastly cough, the unsung part of the famed "voice of Erin." When your day is the spotted reality romanticized in that harp, you sometimes see a leprous whiteness in the fingers straying over the strings.

Tommy Muldoon knew that cough, for it was something as familiar to him as the sound of running water in the kitchen sink, and seemed part of his life. His sister, Kathleen, was for many years in "a decline." He was very young when he first heard that choking; it seemed to him as though her lungs were filled with dry gravel and that the cough was making it tear at her throat. As he grew older he came to think of that sound as something that went quite naturally with his home, just as the wireless went with Johnny Devlin's and the garage with Bill McKeown's, whose father was "rotten with money." It was just part of that "delicacy in the family," about which he heard when the neighbors looked at him and said: "Aye, it's a weary world, God help the gosson." Yes, it was just something in his house, like the wireless or the car or the greyhound or the brass knocker in some other house. It wasn't one of the big things: it had nothing to do with "the Cause," anti-Partition, or injustice to Catholics, so the local Nationalist M.P. knew nothing about it. Her coughing drowned no votes. It was just a cough—God help us—and there were a few hundred other such coughs—God help us again—within a radius of a few miles. It was just something that filled the weary years of a mother, and measured her hours as with a great choking hourglass, desert dry, hopeless.

Tommy was strong—that was one consolation, anyhow. He took after his mother's side, maybe, though it is hard to trace the source; for tuberculosis in Ireland is like a white, leprous finger, always raised and erratically pointing. It was good to see him growing up stout and strong, causing no worries except those incidental to keeping a seat in his trousers and leather under his feet. He had left school with a fine reputation for honesty. If he left no great name for learning there, at least he left his name boldly carved on the back desk: Thomas Joseph Anthony Muldoon, the Confirmation name not being forgotten. It was a bit of a feat to wind all that through the crazy pavement made by other names. But there it was, clear and bold, a snake of crude letters crazily twisting: and having left his name for the wondering and worshiping eyes of future Muldoons, he had given his full attention to the present by taking a job as mill boy under Patch Rafferty.

A clip on the ear and a string of unprintables, on the first day, gave him a pretty clear idea of just how smooth life was to be under Patch. When McCourt went to Newry, Patch would come to the boy and, gripping him roughly by the lapels, he would say:

"I haven't been out, see? I haven't put a foot outside the mill, see? Or, by heavens, I'll shove you into the machine, and who's to prove it wasn't an accident, eh?"

Then he would put on his coat, fumble mysteriously at the back where the money was, and slip quietly out toward the nearest pub. Two hours later he would return, fly into a drunken rage, and swear at the lad for not having finished the work he should have done himself. Once, he had come back in his usual mood, but swearing and railing on a hot day being weary work, he lay down on some old sacks and was soon heavily asleep. The boy had grown to hate him. A huge beam of wood stood against the wall—a new beam which had just been delivered and was to be put in position the following day. It had been placed rather carelessly, and a very little shoulder push would send it over. Patch's head was touching the wall. A little shove with the shoulder—not with the hands, for they always looked for fingerprints—and it would slide along the wall, and then.... But the thought of what *would* happen then made him lose his nerve. Patch Rafferty would never know that his life once hung on the thread of a boy's patience which he himself had pulled taut.

The self-control was rewarded, for Patch's downfall had come quickly after this. It all happened very simply. Farmer Daly had reached the gate and was turning into the road. As ill luck would have it for Patch, McCourt's pony and trap arrived at the same time, and the two men exchanged a few words. The cart seemed very full.

"Took more than your usual four bags, Jimmy?" McCourt asked, nodding to the cart.

"Four, me foot," came the answer. "I never took four. There's always two for us, three for the grocer Ward's, and one to be halved between the Sloans and the Waterses. That's the least I ever took."

McCourt blinked once or twice, but recovered sufficiently to make a few more remarks that served to shield his sudden surprise.

He strode across to the mill, where Patch, who had seen him in time, was working away with a vigor that no man could keep up for more than an hour.

"Patch, show me the last entry in the books."

Patch fumbled among the ledgers, muttered it must be here somewhere, and put up a great show of searching in the hope that McCourt would go away. But it was no good. He stood there, solidly, lips drawn taut in a crisp, ominous line. Finally, he took the book from Patch and found the entry himself.

"Four bags, eh?" he asked, reading it.

"Aye, that's right. Four."

"Funny how two more fell out of the clouds between here and the gate."

"He's a liar. He got no six from me. There was two he had hisself in the cart when he came. Wasn't there, Tommy?"

It sounded like a question, but the accompanying look had the sting of a whip in it. However, the boy had suddenly had quite enough. He took a few precautionary steps nearer the door and said defiantly:

"It *was* six. And it was six always and sometimes more."

Then discretion came elbowing his valor and he took to his heels across the field.

"The little lying—" Patch began.

"That's enough," McCourt cut in acidly. "You have half an hour to get yourself and your belongings out of here. And think yourself lucky that it's not jail for you. But look here! Just you lay one finger on that boy… Come on, get out!"

When the news reached Tommy, he gave vent to his joy by hopping stones off a zinc roof at the back of his house. It made a fine, rattling sound like thunderous applause. At a moment of lull in the rattle, however, a doubt occurred to him. Maybe he would get worse in his place. Better the devil you know than the devil you don't know. But no, that couldn't be. If the head devil himself came, he couldn't be a bigger devil than Patch. He dismissed the doubt by slinging a handful of stones together. They made a fine old rattle, enough to restore the confidence of a retreating army.

"Come on, Tommy, we have got to get to work on this mess.

It was three weeks later, and Tommy's first day under the new miller. It had begun well, for Tommy had been greeted with a smile and a handshake that wasn't the kind of kid stuff other people gave him, but real man-to-man. It made him feel good. He gave him half an orange, and there was something different about that, too. It wasn't given like you were a kid. They sat on two barrels sucking the orange and talking as solidly as if they were behind two pints. So, when the time came to start work, the boy felt that he had suddenly grown up and must work like a man.

At half past six that evening they were still hard at it. At seven, the new miller said to Tommy:

"Righto, lad, we'll pack it up for the night."

Tommy grinned back.

"O.K., boss," he answered, feeling very big.

He felt very tired, too, for, unknown to himself, he had done twice his usual work.

"Tired, lad?" the miller asked, putting on his coat and making for the door. "I'm tired myself. Best look at the fine job we made of this place today. Tomorrow, we'll have customers again."

As they reached the door, it opened and McCourt came in. He looked around the place and whistled with astonishment. It was incredible that such order should have replaced such chaos after only one day's work.

"This is marvelous,'" he said warmly.

The miller pointed to Tommy and said: "Well, that's the one to thank."

"I'll do more than thank," McCourt answered. "Your money goes up by half a crown a week from now on, Tommy, and you just keep this up and there's no knowing what it might rise to."

Yes, it had been a day of wonders. Tommy glowed as he walked with the miller across the field. What harm if he was tired himself. He was happy. There would be no more blows and cursing. Just a busy day of happy work; the joy of knowing that he was being treated like a man; the lift that a rise in pay and brightening prospects bring with them; above all, the joy of working with a man who had already won his love and confidence. There are times when the glitter of the sun on the leaves, like a shower of powdered glass, seems nature's echo to a joy in the heart. Tommy stuck his hands deeply into his pockets, and walked with the firm step of a man who looks on the world and finds it good.

But at the corner of the road, he saw a movement in the hedge and the joy went out of his day. He felt a sudden icy hollow in the pit of his stomach, for he knew that Patch was lurking there, silently waiting. He tried to speak, to warn his new friend of the danger, but his tongue was swollen with fear. Another movement in the hedge, and the tall, lanky figure stepped out on the road.

"Look out. Patch!" Tommy gave the alarm.

Puzzled, the Stranger hesitated for a second, then walked on.

"Your name is Murray?" Patch growled, putting himself directly in his way.

"My name is Murray," came the level answer.

"Well, mine's Rafferty"—said with an intonation calculated to sound the hour of reckoning.

"Well, what can I do for you?"

"Listen to that, now," answered Patch with menacing sarcasm. "What can you do for me? Just this, you filthy, scabbing prig. Get out of that job you sneaked into, when I was out striking for more money from yon tight-fisted, yid-livered McCourt. A living wage, huh? The Pope says I can have that, huh? So get to hell out…"

"I'm no scab and you're no wronged man. I took the job you were sacked from and I'll have no badgering from you!"

What happened next was not very clear to Tommy, for he was rigid with fear. He saw Patch stepping forward, mouth snarling, eyes blazing, fist raised. He saw a peculiar light coming into the Stranger's eyes, a light that was not fear, yet was something like fear. Patch saw it, too—a fear that wasn't a fear, but something strange and impersonal. It spoke suddenly in a crisp command:

"Don't strike!"

The words and the look caused a certain iciness to pass through Patch, and all energy seemed to ebb from the uplifted arm. He was suddenly a very bewildered man. He had found that he could not strike. Impotently, he began to rage at the man before him.

"And look here, Murray, if you cross my path again, I'll…"

He turned on his heel and stamped off. He had not struck the blow, but he felt his hatred hardening like a clenched fist inside him—a cold hatred, which he scarcely understood, against the white-faced man in the road. Patch had met with something which both puzzled and thwarted him, and he hated it with all the energy of his being.

For a few seconds, the Stranger stood looking after him. The blood returned to his face, and except for the throbbing of a prominent vein in his forehead, there was nothing to show his recent danger. Tommy heard him muttering with a kind of suppressed joy:

"He did not strike. Thank God."

Then he turned to the youngster and said brightly:

"Well, Tommy, we must be getting along."

Though he had been but a short time in the little town, it was obvious, from the friendly words and greetings he received as they walked along together, that the town had accepted him. Certainly, the children of the town had accepted him, indeed had already claimed him for their own. The wise grown-up heads liked him, but puzzled over him; the children loved him and were unconscious of any puzzle. Adult eyes are dim with the dust of disillusionment left by impressions of white souls which later proved whited sepulchers; and they have learned to trust the vision of a child, in the belief that earth's nearest thing to angelic intuition is the clean glance of a child. This Stranger, who had come so quietly among them, already gave the impression of an amiable shadow communing with itself, having no more vital contact with the life about him than the passing caress of a shadow on a sunlit wall. Wise heads had nodded over him, and wise theories were put forward to explain that guardedness, amounting to a carefully kept aura of mystery, which they sensed in the few words they had managed to exchange with him. The most subtle leading questions had been answered with a skilled evasiveness which left the questioner with knowledge which, analyzed, proved to be exactly what he knew before. Thus the Stranger became, in the popular imagination, an I.R.A. organizer for a day, a B special for half a day, a private detective for quite three days until his lack of interest in everything made such an idea ridiculous. By the end of the week the river of inventiveness had run dry, and he was allowed his coveted anonymity as a kind of shadow walking in a mist that had voices of secret sorrow in it. The town received him for his kindness to the children, with whom the last word in the matter was very wisely left.

The children's verdict was given in the happy smiles that greeted him, and in the fine chat they had for him. John Molloy, reputed the longest head in the village, had sought a clue to the mystery by getting within earshot of some children with whom the Stranger had stopped to speak. What he heard was a child talking with children, and he went away with a strange feeling that was partly acute shame at having eavesdropped, and partly a vague feeling of something lovely and wonderful. Moreover, the Stranger was known to attend Mass and receive Holy Communion devoutly every morning, and it was felt among the townsfolk that a man whose first waking hour was ambrosial with Divinity had the whiteness of manna in his heart. And yet—there was a mystery in that, too. Why should a man, who was so obviously "hand-in-glove with them above," take such pains to avoid the priest? It was obvious on more than one occasion that he did so, and this had not escaped the notice of the priest himself. There was, for instance, the day when the Stranger had seen him through the window of McGough's kitchen, opening the front gate, and had risen abruptly and made for the stairs door leading to his room. Another time, the priest had heard him closing the back kitchen door when he had entered the house, though he was convinced, the Stranger had been in the room a moment before. To the good people of the town, this seemed as wonderful as if a piece of steel should fly from the magnet. The priest thought his own thoughts and kept his own counsel....

The pair of tired workers arrived at Tommy's house, and as though to emphasize the fact for the poor lad, sounds of a strangling cough came from within. The Stranger was about to bid Tommy a cheery "Well, lad, till tomorrow" when those sounds made him pause.

"Maybe I'd better go in and have a word with your mother. I could tell her what a man-and-a-half you are for work."

Tommy glowed and led the way to the open door. It gave straight into a little kitchen-cum-living room, dominated on one side by a huge picture of the Sacred Heart, and on the other by a picture of St. Theresa of the Child Jesus. It was fitting that her image should be here, for she died of tuberculosis and must therefore be particularly tender toward those prayers which rise up to her, torn and raddled with that crucifying cough. Between the two pictures stood Mrs. Muldoon, busily kneading bread. Her face had the lines of life scratched on its beauty, but the smile with which she came forward, shyly wiping her hands in her apron, had a bravery in it.

"It's a pleasure to meet you, Mr. Murray," she greeted, offering her hand and making the ghost of what was once a lovely curtsey in a more gracious age. "Tommy has been telling me about you. And so has Deirdre. Faith and it's you that has a way with them."

He laughed quietly.

"A child's joy is like the ripple of a river over stones: it keeps us from becoming wizened and dry," he answered. "Anyhow, here's Tommy back with the appetite of two elephants, and well he might have for he did six men's work today."

"He's a good lad," she answered, with that curious mixture of modesty and blushing pride with which only a mother can respond to a compliment.

"And what's more, Ma," he added eagerly. "I'm getting a rise of two and six."

"You are, now," she said warmly. "Isn't God good?"

"Aye, Ma," he countered, "and McCourt's not so bad either."

They laughed at this sally. Tommy had a hard streak of the practical in him somewhere.

In the lull that followed, a weak voice called for Tommy. They heard the girl struggling for breath in the grip of a thick cough. Tommy had excused himself and had gone up to her. They stood in silence until the last twist and heave of phlegm marked the end of a spasm, and they knew that the girl had lain back on her pillow, panting, exhausted, pummeled, with the rose-pink flush on her cheek, its loveliness like a mockery. The smile had ebbed from the mother's face, and the lines had suddenly deepened.

"Kathleen," she murmured. "Sure, it's the will of God, but God knows it's hard. Hard. When I hear her cough like that, Mr. Murray, I stand here, and I feel my own soul twisted with two dry and bitter hands that have never a prayer in them. And then I turn to Him"—nodding to the Sacred Heart picture— "and ask Him not to heed a poor woman's foolishness. She's only one of them, you know. I had a lovely son called Patrick Dominic, and the horrible thing got its dry fingers on him, too. I mind the day they eased the coffin round the narrow bend of them stairs. Aisy, now—I mind Johnny Smith saying—I'll go first. But sure, wasn't it me poor, lovely son that had gone first, the light of Christ on him this day! If himself had been alive itself. But sure, wasn't himself the first in this house to make the hard turning of the bend in the stairs...."

She was standing looking at the stairs as though she saw her memories come alive in the shadows there. Then she started suddenly and said:

"But I'm forgetting myself. That's no way to welcome a visitor. It's like a missioner said one time—'A broken spirit dries the bones.' Sometimes I feel like that—dry and weary trying not to be bitter."

As she said this, she looked up at the Stranger before her. She felt suddenly like a person, racked with thirst and complaining to God, who looks up and sees a fountain of limpid water. For the quiet, intense sympathy of the eyes meeting hers was as a cool sprinkle on a burning face.

A strange thought had struck him, as he listened to her and felt the dryness of her sorrow. Her sorrow was another of those great knots, as dry as if woven with corpse hair, that make the tangle of human life. Only at the Final Judgment will that tangle be turned to show the beauty that was woven of human pain. In that turning, the ways of God to women like Mrs. Muldoon—yes, and to men like himself—will be justified; and human suffering, with a new splendor of meaning, will find a glorious place in the human story as man's filling up of what was lacking to the lifting up on Calvary. But meantime, the sufferers must grope their way and know the dryness. It was thoughts like these that crowded the eyes that looked so sympathetically at Mrs. Muldoon. She felt a strange power in those eyes. They were filled with sympathy for her sorrow, but there was something else in them, too; something she could not fathom, but which she knew in a rush of fresh hope.

Tommy had come down again. He looked at his mother with a gentleness that is most lovely when found in the manner of a growing boy toward his mother.

"She's all right now, Mother, and I've given her a drink."

"Thanks, lad," she answered quietly.

He had waited to have a cup of tea and to chat with Tommy and his mother. Tommy had eaten his way through a substantial hillock of mashed potatoes with a fine pool of meaty gravy crowning it; had followed this with thick wedges of bread and marmalade, washed down with a man-size mug of good, strong tea, and was soon on his way to watch a football match in a field nearby. Deirdre had come in and had her tea. She was a beautiful child, with eyes that echoed the blue loveliness of her mother's, and fair hair that fell with the gentleness of soft rain about her shoulders, a thousand lights in it when she tossed her head. Her face was an unusual mixture of doll-like loveliness and the elements of a strong character. Her mother used to wonder some-times at the "queer bit of a temper" she had, but she liked it in her, because it went with other qualities which would be excellent assets in the battle of life. The child was ordinarily shy with visitors but not with this one. Her face lit up with joy when she saw him sitting in her own kitchen drinking tea—an honor which would make all her little companions envious of her—and she came and chatted gaily with him. He heard all the sayings and doings of her day, and indeed it was her mother who felt herself the third. Deirdre then went toward the stairs, but before she got there, her mother said:

"Better not, Deirdre. She's not so good today."

It was always like this. The comfort of the chatter in the kitchen, then something to remind them of their sorrow and chill them.

"Well, Mother," the little one said, "can I have ten minutes more out?"

Her bright coming and her cheery words as she ran out were a ripple of joy in the room.

"Aye, she's a clip, that one," she laughed affectionately.

"She's cheerful and she's plucky," he answered, "two things which will see her through life very well indeed. You said something a while ago, Mrs. Muldoon, about a broken spirit drying the bones. Well, I know the first part of that saying, and it is—'A merry heart acts like a medicine.' When you feel the dry, let the wee one's laugh ripple over you, as I said a while ago, like water on dry stones. For I believe God often sugars the pills of our sorrow with the laughter of a child."

They sat in silence watching the fire. He felt nervous, for he had not yet come to what had caused him to break his journey. He began, as though each word was gingerly feeling its way:

"About the girl upstairs—Kathleen, I mean—I was thinking, maybe…"

She sensed his awkwardness, and met it with a smile.

"You were going to say that I should get her to a hospital, were you?" she asked.

"Well, yes, something like that," he answered.

"Indeed, I've often sat and thought of that. But what's the use. Thinking is a weary business when you have no money to get past the thinking. If she could get out of the country, she might mend."

"I was thinking, maybe," he went on hesitantly, "if someone could, were to take on to send…"

"Aye," she said, "there's many's the poor neighbor round here would do that for me if they could. But not any of the moneyed ones. They say when the money gets into a man it makes a stone of him."

"Look, Mrs. Muldoon,", he asked suddenly, "would you do me a big favor?"

"Well, now, there's a thing to ask. Of course, of course."

"Will you let me send Kathleen to Frimley Sanatorium in England, and pay for her?"

The mother looked at him in amazement. This great kindness offered as though it was a favor sought, absolutely overwhelmed her.

"Ah, Mr. Murray," she answered, "that wouldn't be just a matter of five pounds or so. It would take a lot—a big lot. But you don't know the lift it is to me to know there's still such kindness in the world."

"I'm sure I can manage," he went on. "You see, I've a bit in the post office I haven't touched for many years. It should be a tidy bit now and I won't be needing it. I'm paid good money at the mill and I'll be getting commission on sales. That's much more than I'll ever need."

"But I couldn't let you…"

"It's for Kathleen. She's only eighteen. She'll have the fight of the young in her."

"No, I couldn't. It wouldn't be…"

"Please. I ask it as a favor."

A fit of coughing cut jaggedly across their conversation, and the mother relented.

"Well, God and His Mother bless you for it!" she said.

"Well, well, that's fine," he said, with evident satisfaction. "But one big favor more. I do this on one condition. You must not breathe a word about who did it. Promise me."

It went hard on her to have to do so.

When Deirdre came in, she found her mother sitting alone in the kitchen.

"Ah," she said, "is Mr. Murray gone? I thought maybe he might be here still. He's a lovely man."

"Aye, he's all that, he's all that!"

In spite of herself, there were tears in her voice.

"You're crying, Mother. What's the matter?"

"Nothing, Deirdre, nothing," she answered. "I was just sitting here thinking."

Back in the little pink room, the Stranger looked out at the peace that lay on field and hill. There was a look of abstraction in his face as though he pondered many things that had the warp of pain and the woof of sorrow in them. Then, turning from the window, he murmured:

"Thank God, he did not strike."

He went on his knees at the bedside, and buried his face in his hands.

He had scarcely noticed the flowers arranged with such care on the window ledge.

CHAPTER THE FOURTH

Father Seumas Sheridan was a priest who liked to feel that his flock looked to him in every need with candor and with confidence. He could not bear a face averted from him or a look of servility or of fear. Not that he was a coward, for a well-founded legend existed in the village which left no doubts on that score. It would seem that a certain character in the district had made himself a menace to its morals and good name, and he had been denounced from the altar for his misdeeds by Father Seumas, who was the curate at that time. Retaliation had taken the form of tipsy soliloquies in various locals about men who snipe from behind Roman collars, and what would be done with them if they hadn't a collar to skulk behind. This, it would seem, went on for some time, until a certain moonlit night when, on a white stretch of road, two bicycles were approaching each other. Father Seumas, mounted on one of them, saw the other coming, and quickly dismounted. With a sudden wrench he removed his collar and put it on the grass. He was removing his coat quietly when the other came up.

"Well, my good man," the priest had challenged him, "there's no collar to skulk behind now, so let's meet as man to man."

The story went on to say that seldom in the history of the parish was a bicycle ridden so swiftly. For one look at the magnificent physique emerging from that coat was enough to set those wheels spinning as if a legion of devils was in the hub of each wheel. The incident would have missed its place in the folklore but for the fact that Red Kearney came roaring along on his motorcycle, dipping down the hill and shooting to the crest of the next as though rebounding, to reach the crest in time to see the whole thing. The effect had been salutary, for the following Saturday saw the culprit— waiting his turn in the confession queue. One of the village wits said that he had pedaled and pedaled around and around the village, until he pedaled to the box.

Clerical legends in Ireland rival in number the black-berries on her bushes, and the embroidery of fiction about them can be as ingenious and as intricate as the most riotous moments in Celtic ornamentation. It is always true, however, that the quality embedded in the embroidery is really to be founded in the man about whom the fact-and-fiction web is spun. Therefore, while some questioned the accuracy of detail, none questioned the courage of the man about whom the story was told. It was certain, then, that Father Seumas would not shy from the mystery in a situation that might involve a duty for him.

He often thought of this Stranger who lived so quietly

among the people—going to daily Mass and then immersing himself in his work at the mill, to emerge in the evening for long, lonely walks over fields and hills. Mrs. McGough had told the priest that on several occasions when they asked him what direction he had taken, he had seemed at a loss for a moment, and then he would say something like:

"Yes, it must have been the North road; I remember seeing the old tower."

Of one thing Mrs. McGough knew nothing. She didn't have an inkling of how he spent his half day or his long Sunday afternoon. All she knew was that he took some sandwiches and set off on an old bicycle he had bought, taking a different direction each time and not returning until nightfall. There was always something bulky in his pocket as well on these occasions. These bits of information volunteered to him were of little interest to Father Sheridan. What did interest him and trouble him was the fact that this man was so obviously avoiding him. There was more than the flying corner of a coat glimpsed in a closing door. There had been the Sunday afternoon when they nearly met at the crossroads but for a sudden swerve to the right which the Stranger made, though he had given every indication of going straight on. He had saluted the priest, some fifty yards off, and pedaled quickly down the hill. It was well known, of course, that, while the Stranger was affable and friendly, he certainly kept people at arm's length from anything that in the least veered toward the personal. But where a priest was concerned, he was positively furtive.

One Thursday—the half day at the mill—something had happened which had the effect of putting an edge on the priest's whole attitude. It was the day of old Canon Power's funeral. The air was murky under a sky like churned mud, when they laid the body of this splendid priest in the ground, and the clay that fell on the coffin was thickened with the driving rain. Father Seumas stood listening to its thud, for it sounded like dull words spoken from the hollowness that this death had made in his life. There would be no more hours of splendid companionship with this priest; no more hours when you felt the kindness of the man like a great warmth about you and your soul expanded to measure itself to the richness of his mind; no more hours when the tension of a thousand worries, held taut in you, were relaxed in the full-throated laugh that greeted his stories—stories with the authentic suds of human nature clinging thickly to them. It was good, Father Seumas thought, to have been privileged to know the richness of this priest. After the funeral, he had returned to the canon's presbytery for a few moments, and in the library he had found his breviary fallen from the edge of the shelf and lying face downward on the floor, its contents scattered. When picking them up, he noticed a little card, carefully printed in the canon's neat lettering, which read:

Your people doze over your
Pealing Pulpit Periods:
But they watch your feet:
They listen to your deeds.

It might serve as epitaph for the canon, he thought, as he slipped the card reverently into his own book, for it summed up the man who had always been reverenced for his deeds.

"Every man's death diminished me," wrote John Donne: and certainly Father Seumas Sheridan felt that life had been narrowed for him by the loss of his friend. There was a meal after the funeral, but he had not the heart to stay for it. The heavy thud of that wet clay might have been his own heart-beats, dull and comfortless, and he preferred to be alone with them. He could have got a lift in a car—his own was laid up for repairs—but he preferred to push his way against a sullen, sodden head wind, along the six-mile road that led to his parish. About three miles on, a little road ran into the main road, and its hill was crowned by a small church. From where he rode along, a little stained-glass window showed in the center of the apse: its color in all its grayness was like a bright word spoken quietly; and it spoke of the priest he had seen lowered into the clay, for it was a Harry Clarke window he had put there, of which he had been proud. Father Sheridan felt a great impulse to pray there, as in a place that held some-thing very personal to his friend, and he dismounted from his bicycle and climbed the steep hill. The deserted church was very quiet, there was a certain clamminess about the seats, and dusk hung in the air, making a flickering beacon of the little lamp swinging slightly in the sanctuary. He knelt down and soon found the peace of the silence seeping through him.

As his eyes became accustomed to the half-light, the shadows began to recede, so that he could discern objects in the church more clearly. To his surprise, he discovered that he was not the only worshiper, for a motionless figure knelt to the left of the altar. There might be light enough to read, if a person had been there for a long time and if the book being read was very familiar to the reader. With a start of surprise, he recognized the Stranger of his own parish. So this was the secret of his long evenings away, and of the different directions chosen. Journey's end in every case was the obscurity of a remote church. The priest remained for some time and then rose to go. He hesitated for a second. Ought he to speak to him? This was certainly a fine opportunity. He walked up the church, watching the kneeling figure. It never moved. Then he came near enough to see the face, and he stopped, very still and with the sudden feeling of being a trespasser.

Sorrow and a strange peace molded the face; it might have been a gentle, gracious face formed of the shadow about him. He knelt alone with some secret, and only in the silence of the church could he find ease from the sorrow in it. The priest had come here to be alone with his sorrow, and he had found another soul with another burden. He would feel it as a desecration of silence and sorrow to speak. And yet, it was hard not to do so, for he felt a kind of bond between them— the bond of two thirsty men who meet at the same fountain. He knelt down a few seats behind him.

As he did so, his heel struck the seat. The Stranger started, went rigid, and, with a quick movement, closed and lifted the open book that had lain on the seat before him. The priest wondered whether he had been recognized. He certainly seemed suddenly on his guard against something. Against what or against whom? Against the priest, was it? Father Sheridan was hurt to think so. He hesitated, again, between two minds, then he rose, genuflected, and turned to leave the church. As he turned, he again saw the face of the Stranger. It was very pale, showing white even in the surrounding grayness. As the priest went down the church toward the door, he felt that the very air about the kneeling figure was sighing its relief.

He puzzled over the whole matter as he continued his way home. What was the meaning of this furtive piety, as carefully hidden as another might keep his vices? Why that quick and frightened—yes, there could be no doubt about it, frightened—concealing of the book. What book? Suddenly he stopped pedaling, alert with an idea that had just come to him. Could it be possible that...but no, it couldn't. There was no need to get melodramatic about it.

The following day, Father Sheridan could not rid his mind of the incident of the previous evening. It distracted him in the celebration of Mass; it showed itself in various lights as he read his Office, rising from the Psalms as though some of the words were a comment on it. By the time he had finished his breakfast, he was determined to find occasion, in a very full program, to visit the mill at a time when this man simply could not avoid meeting him.

He cycled into the little town. Dusk was beginning to huddle the houses together as if, like their occupants, they had come cozily together to exchange cozy little bits of gossip in the smoke of their chimneys. The rain had ceased and a fresh wind had blown up from the south. The air felt as if it had been newly washed. The gas lamps had been lighted and they stood, four-faced on their gaunt bodies, along the street, splashing a watery ocher on the evening like great blots of ink dropped in a regular line on gray blotting paper. Squares of light on the pavement marked the position of the public houses, and where their doors were open, fingers of malt and whisky fumes caressed the air. A lone cart came rumbling along the street, the driver asleep with the reins on his knees, the horse making its own drowsy way home. Father Seumas loved the atmosphere of it all, which seemed always to have that same calm, peaceful welcome for him when he returned. It was as balm to a hurt mind.

Balm to a hurt mind? The idea seemed to refocus for him that quiet, secretly suffering face he had seen in the still church. What wound had the soul of this man suffered that he had come here to ease its pain in the peace the little town promised—to draw the festering matter with the poultice of its soothing silence? He wished he could do something for him; for what, he pondered, was the priesthood, save a mystical two-edged sword—one edge tempered to the lancing of festering soul sores. But what could he do, when this man seemed to be avoiding him always and everywhere?

In the shadow of the tree the old Proleek miniature showed wet and slimy, and there was moisture on the face of his Brigid as though she wept for the sorrows of her people. He saw them both when he lighted his lamp and went to draw the curtains. There was silence about him, except for the sibilant hiss of the lamp. It might have been the whispering of a thousand secret sorrows in the great heart of an unheeding and indifferent world. He reached for a book, and, as he opened it, a newspaper cutting, already yellowing with age, slipped from among its pages and fluttered unnoticed to the ground. He had a habit of keeping cuttings in his books—strange cuttings that few others would find significant. It lay on the rug, half concealed by his chair. He had put a match to his fire and the flames were already leaping to throw a shadow dance of chair, of book, of priest on the walls, which was like a harlequin backcloth to the most somber moments of Hamlet. For nothing danced at that moment in the mind of Father Seumas. The wind of the spirit that blew in the secret places of him was a dry and lonely one, catching the thorny things of life and flinging them into a tearing tangle. The leaping flames picked out the letters of a glaring headline on the piece of paper under his feet, but there were no eyes to read it. The eyes that might have read it were closed in a heavy, tired torpor.

At first it was a dreamless one, but it soon filled with a grotesque medley of sounds and voices. The wet thud of the clay fell heavily through it, the thickened lumps falling, now on the coffin, now on the stained-glass window of the church which somehow lay in the place of the coffin lid. He watched with hands of horror clamped to his mouth, to see the stained-glass crack and sliver in the blows. It didn't break, but the colors dissolved into each other, and the face of his dead friend looked at him as through a sheet of glass. Then the dead eyes came alive for a second, and looked significantly to his right. Turning in wonder, he saw the Stranger beside him, his face ashen, drawn, corpselike. Then the whole thing dissolved into a red-flecked grayness, the playing of the fire through the film of his half-opened eyes. He woke to find his brow clammy and cold.

The lamp had gone down and was spluttering its gasp of light fitfully through the room. It seemed to have the effect of prolonging the nightmare into the realms of consciousness. He rose quickly, replenished it, and lighted it again. He sighed in relief, as though its steady light were the symbol and guarantee of a consciousness in which coffin lids could not become stained glass, nor stained glass dissolve into the lines of a human face. He attempted to read, to steady his mind with the deep, calm thought of his author, but in vain. Words, words, words, registering nothing. There was no remedy for it but to close the book and surrender to the thoughts that were crowding the air between the print and his brain, filtering the author's words through a crazy sieve of his own sorrow, doubt, and fear, so that they reached him white and meaningless. For a long time he sat there, gazing into the fire. Then he rose suddenly, put on his hat and coat, and went out.

He went into the town, passed the spot where Mooney the vet was found hanging from a tree, passed the haunted well, and came into the main street of irregular houses linking pub to pub. The street was practically deserted, and a few cats were beginning to proclaim that the night was theirs. When Father Seumas was some twenty yards from McGough's, the Stranger turned the corner ahead of him and dismounted at the door. The mantle in the lamp near the priest was broken, and the light it gave was an ineffectual splutter. He stepped into the deeper shade of a great yard door, and stood perfectly still. He watched the Stranger dismounting. The light from the lamp at McGough's shone full on his face. It was not the face of the priest's dream: it was not even the face he had seen in the shadows of the quiet church. Father Seumas suddenly felt as though he had been caught in some disgraceful eavesdropping. He also began to wonder whether his seventy years were leaving him more open to inroads from the fantastic in all its forms. Standing in the shadows of that gate, the question that had been trembling, unasked, at the threshold of his consciousness, now seemed utterly crazy and fantastic. Dare he put the question to this Stranger and still keep his claim to be considered a sane man? Yet he took this strange fantasy to rest with him, and it remained to trouble his dreams.

There are few things so ruthless as the manner in which the first waking hour deals with the fears and enthusiasms of the previous night. The result of "sleeping on it" can be devastating: as soon might a person think of reaching through the darkness to recapture, in morning garishness, the colors of the sunset. Father Seumas had hoped for this, but he was disappointed. The morning did indeed bring its customary blunting, but the urge to see this man remained acute, the urge to put to him a dangerous—yes, let him admit it honestly, a delirious—question. Even that most prosaic stretch that lies between the morning hours of eleven and twelve did not kill that urge; and so it came about that the querulous chimes from the market-house clock at half past eleven found Father Seumas hesitating near that corner from which Patch Rafferty had sneered, and then continuing toward the gate that led to the mill, his mind made up.

He had come at a slack moment, for the last cart of the morning custom had pulled out on the road just before he reached the gate. The door was open and he stepped inside. Standing by the window, absorbed in his ledger, the Stranger did not notice his arrival, so that the priest had an opportunity of studying the face quietly for a moment. It was a fine, clear profile, with a soft purity and innocence in it, even though the face was absorbed in a concentration of soulless figures, which often gives to a man's features the hard edges of a coin.

"Good morning, Mr. Murray," he greeted him.

The Stranger started, and looked at him. For a second the priest saw a peculiar look on the face that was part fear, part defensiveness, giving the impression that this man considered himself cornered at last. About what? And by whom? The look passed in a second, but it was sufficient to give the priest that oppressiveness—almost despondency—which he always experienced when he met defensive reserves in souls committed to him. He met all his people with openness and sincerity; it hurt him to meet with anything that savored of the opposite in return, and especially from this man, who already enjoyed the esteem and confidence of the whole town but who seemed to have singled out the priest as the only one to be avoided. The Stranger stepped forward with a smile that might well have made the preceding second seem an illusion of light, and gripped the priest's hand in welcome.

Father Sheridan was sensitive to handshakes, as such a man might well have been whose own handshake might fittingly serve as the norm of them all. There was the man who would lay his hand in yours, so that you had the impression of a cold, dead fish lying on your palm, and you registered a colorless, flabby creature in the man who greeted you. There was the strong vise grip, dangerous to some dozen bones, which told you that here was a big, self-willed, generous, passionate, and narrow man, whose virtues and vices were all authentic but had the uncertainty of the two sides of a spinning coin. Then there was the firm, warm, dry grip that had just the right amount of pressure in it, that stayed just long enough in the palm, without the insincerity of the two-fingered, pseudo-refined butterfly flutter, nor the suspicious lingering grip which makes you think that the owner, like the hand he offered, was inclined to protest too much. Father Sheridan recognized, in the hand gripping his own, the qualities that went with refinement of character from nature and grace.

"You are welcome, Father," he said simply.

The priest looked about him, impressed by the many evidences of hard and properly ordered work.

"You have certainly made an excellent job of this place," he complimented him, "and I hear that the quality of your flour is now so good that the carts are coming long distances to fetch it."

"Well, Father," he answered, "it is really easy with such new machinery as we have here."

"Patch didn't make much of a fist of it," the priest laughed. "The poor devil came to me one night when the whisky had made him sorry for himself, and asked me to see McCourt and that maybe he might take him back. Patch is a boyo who has no time for me when he's sober, but anyhow I went to see McCourt next day. McCourt's answer was to bring me along to see the condition of the mill, and when I saw it, there could be only one answer."

"Aye," the Stranger replied, "there was a lot of work before we could get under our steam. And I would never have got through it, I believe, except for Tommy's help. He's a fine lad."

"Aye, and a changed one," the priest added. "He was getting morose and furtive in his ways through contact with Patch—not at all like the lad who had organized the poltergeist scare a few years ago." The priest laughed as he remembered how many had been taken in by it. "But since he came under you, he certainly has regained his liveliness and spunk."

"He's a good lad," came the answer, "and what's more, he'll soon be as good as I am myself. Look at that flour, now. That's his work. I'm keeping it to show McCourt if he drops in this evening. I want him to see just how good he is."

"Why?" the priest asked suddenly.

The Stranger appeared not to have heard, and the priest sensed the smallest hint of the old guardedness. A signed receipt lay open on the desk and the priest picked it up. The signature was an educated one, beautiful, every letter full of character.

"You write a good hand, Michael," he commented, "which makes me guess that perhaps you have had a good education? It has the flow of a man who has done much more than sign receipts."

"Yes," he admitted, "I got a good education."

The priest felt that all this beating about the bush was getting him nowhere. Why not take the opportunity that might not recur, and ask the question that had been troubling him?

"I really came to ask a question, which I hope you'll forgive me for asking, for it's rather a blunt question," he began.

But at that moment a cheerful whistling came from the left, and Tommy began to climb down the ladder. The tune he whistled was one of those which are as at home in an Irish country street as on Broadway, so effectively has Americanism steamrolled the native tastes of Europe. He turned around at the bottom, his rosy face glowing, his clothes and cap thick with flour dust, giving the impression of a ghost with a rush of blood to its head. The opportunity had passed for putting the question, and behind the politeness of the man, the priest sensed a well-controlled surge of relief.

"Do you know, Michael," the boy began.

Then he saw the priest and became a bit self-conscious. He touched his cap to him.

"Well, Tommy lad," the priest greeted him, "but it's you that's looking fresh and well. As a matter of fact, you're getting so fresh and lively that I suppose we may be expecting another noisy ghost around the town anytime now."

Tommy felt a little uncomfortable, but the hearty laugh that went with it put him at his ease.

"Anyhow," he went on, "you look like a ghost yourself now, with all that flour on you. Why, if your own mother saw you near the oven this minute, she'd pop you right in. All you would want to do to make another scare would be to stand out on the road just as you are, under Mooney's tree maybe, and there are people who would swear they saw a ghost with a face of fire."

They laughed together.

"I'm getting great news of you, Tommy. Michael here tells me you are getting to be a fine miller yourself."

"I'm not so bad," the boy conceded, "but anyone could be as good who got as good teaching."

"I don't know so much about that," the Stranger answered. "But one thing I do know is that if ever I leave, you'll be well able to take my place."

"But you're not thinking of going?" the boy asked, and the anxiety in his voice would be a glowing tribute to any man.

"No, I hope not," came the answer, "but you never know."

The rumble of a cart on the stones outside, and a shout from its occupant, put an end to the conversation. The priest held out his hand and felt the same authentic grip.

"Well, Michael," he said, "it's been nice seeing you and your Sancho Panza, and I hope to have the same pleasure soon again."

"You are welcome at any time, Father," he answered.

In spite of his warmth and politeness, the priest again felt a well-controlled relief, a relaxing of tension through the whole man. A less observant person than this keen priest would have missed it; he noticed it, and it hurt him deeply.

He crossed the field, his brow clouded with his troubled thoughts. Why had he not put his question sooner? Or was it really a good thing that the lad had butted in to prevent him making a fool of himself? At the gate, he paused and looked back at the scene. Murray was out, briskly helping to load the sacks on the cart. Everything was solid and real— the mill, the horse and cart, the three men loading. Was this the reality, and if so, why couldn't he dismiss that nagging question and accept the plain situation of a man who wished to live quietly and was shy of a Roman collar? In the clear, common sense light of noon, the question was just an absurd fancy. And yet he knew that when the silence of night gathered about him and his lamp's low hiss, like the voice of quiet sorrow, filled the room, the question would return, insistent, nagging, not to be dismissed....

The winter sun sank in a blotched and angry sky which heralded a storm. Not a wicked storm, but one of those petulant affairs of gusty winds and heavy, driving rain which comes from the sky in great, unbroken spines of water. The little town had adjourned to its hearths, its pubs, and its cinema, leaving the little street free to the flinging wind and the warming drops it carried. A great, black cloud was hastening the gathering of darkness. The wind careened through the street, met the rising ground, and rose gaily to wash like a river of air around a little cottage perched near the top of the hillock. The Newry road breasted that hillock and a short, rough path led to the house. The light went out in the window as though the wind had extinguished it, and Old Tom—one of the best known characters in the district—pushed his way out against the wind, his clothes flung about him like a blown scarecrow. He locked the door carefully behind him. It was a Friday night, and every Friday night Old Tom visited his sister's son down at the forge. It would take more than a fistful of wind and rain to keep him from doing so. Pushing busily with his stick as though it were a third leg, he made his way down the path and on to the road.

When on occasion in various pubs, he had spoken and boasted of a certain sum of money he was gathering for a certain purpose, Old Tom had not noticed a long, big-boned, fiery-headed man standing quietly in the corner, apparently absorbed in his thoughts and really missing not a syllable. He had not noticed how this same man had hung about the street watching to see what pub he would enter that he might follow him and take up his usual abstracted stand at the bar. Nor did he notice a slight flicker of those thick, red eyelashes on the night when, a little over-mellowed with drink, he had told his companions how, every Thursday, some money came to him, how he cashed it and put it with the rest. He had said enough. The following Thursday, that same thin lath of a man was crouched in the bushes, watching every move. It was dusk, and the old man had lighted his lamp. He rose into view in the yellow patch of light, holding his lamp. The light moved into the other room and then disappeared. Quickly the man emerged from the hedge, and, bending low, he ran to the back of the house. There was a little attic window there, and he was just in time to see the light leaving it. So far, everything had gone smoothly.

The following night, Old Tom again failed to see the crouching figure in the hedge, though he could have touched him as he passed. When the coast was quite clear, the lank figure crept quickly and furtively toward the house. There was neither man nor bird nor beast in sight and dusk had thickened about the hillock, but this man took no chances: he took all the precautions of a daylight robbery. Great, thick pieces of cardboard were tied about his boots to destroy the-footprints, and he wore a pair of rubber gloves. He had already studied the door, and he knew that, while the lock was good and sound, the other side of the door was very suited to his purpose. A little chiseling, a little careful lever-ing, and the fortress was his. He crept quietly forward, feeling his way before him lest he should knock against anything, though he might have overturned everything there without the least danger of raising the alarm. It was hard to negotiate the ladder stairs with the cardboard camouflage on his boots, but he managed it; and once in the attic, the rest was a matter of a few minutes, for the old man's idea of a safe hiding place was naïve in the extreme.

Back on the road, he set off briskly toward Newry. Another heavy shower had begun, and when the headlights of a car cut flickering cones of light through it, he took a chance and hailed the driver. You can't plan a thing perfectly; the element of chance and luck must come in somewhere. It was impossible to distinguish car or driver, and if he was recognized, his alibi was lamed. Luck was with him. The car pulled up, and the face of a total stranger looked out at him.

"Could you lift me to Newry? I have urgent business there and I took a chance of getting a lift."

"Sure," came the answer in that soft Tipperary accent which somehow calls up a vision of mashed potatoes and melted butter. "Hop in."

On the way, he discovered that this was a traveler from Clonmel on his way home from Belfast via Dublin. Nothing could be nicer. He felt the notes thick and crisp against his chest and the silver sang sweetly in his pocket when he rattled it. At Newry, he parted from the traveler, having slipped him half a crown to have a drink. The man thanked him, and put the coin in his pocket. Business was not brisk, money didn't roll as far as it used to, he had a wife and four kiddies, and every little helped. He could not be blamed for not having caught the whiff of the sere cloth, the odor of the candles and of the red, heaped soil from something as innocent as a shining coin.

The robbery and the getaway had taken only twenty minutes. It was only a matter of another three to get himself into a pub where he knew he would invariably find some of his townsfolk on a Friday night. They had never much of a welcome for him, but tonight he seemed anxious to have a word with them all. After a while, he produced a bottle of Irish Mist—the dream liquor of Irish whiskies—and furtively helped his neighbors to some of it. It was stuff that could be got only "at the other side." It seems he had just come from Dundalk—yes, there was a bus, nothing had been overlooked—and had smuggled it with him.

On the whole, Patch Rafferty had had a very successful night. A few more fools like Old Tom in these parts and mill or miller wouldn't worry him. Not that he wouldn't get even with that holy Willie of a craw thumper who had taken his place. No fear of that. Patch Rafferty had never left a job of vengeance incomplete yet.

The night settled into great washes of sultry rain. It ran on the glass of the presbytery window, where the priest stood, pondering many things. It made a cool running river on the window of the little pink room at the back of McGough's, where in just such weather a few nights later, a broken man would sit holding his hope dead in his arms as Mary held her Son.

It washed the grime from the window where Patch Rafferty stood drinking contentedly as a man does who feels that the world is good.

CHAPTER THE FIVE

Nell's attention to the cleaning and polishing of the little pink room and her careful arrangement of flowers in it did not escape the observant eyes of Mrs. McGough. It did not please her, for, in a town like this, one couldn't be too careful.

Conversation—or "talk," as it is more eloquently called—in a small town is no mere exchange of ideas. You must think of it as a long thread of gossamer flung out from a chance word in the street, and eagerly caught up to be ingeniously spun into an intricate web of fact, fiction, and sheer delirium, linking hearth to hearth and pub to pub. Events are embroidered, actions are interpreted, motives are sought— and sometimes the result would make La Rochefoucauld's maxims seem, by comparison, a flattery of human nature. Men's motives are never pitched lower than in the gossip of a small town; and when it is an Irish town, slander and detraction can make a curious cocktail with rosaries and piety. "Well, now you know the kind he is," the old lady is reputed to have said to her crony on the cathedral steps, "and if you wait a wee minute—I'm going in to light a candle—I'll tell you more about him when I come out…"

Mrs. McGough had no illusions about it all. She knew a gossamer thread could curl about you at any moment, and you would find yourself the center of the web. There was one window in a big white house situated at a strategic point in the town, and a face lurked constantly behind a curtain there—which revealed more than the bland face knew—with such consistency that you might have thought it just an illusion of light and shade if you did not know the mind of its owner. The window was well placed with relation to a certain pub; and hence some far-flung "drinking-like-a-fish" streamers through the town. But although tippling streamers were the special interest of the face at the window, the eyes sometimes altered the focus of interest a little to take in such detail as the animated fashion in which a good-looking girl chatted and laughed with the lodger in her house, as they passed the ever-watching window. A rose-tinted thread of gossamer was soon curling through the talk of the little town.

It curled around Mrs. McGough as she returned from paying her wholesaler, and it became a web spun around her when she met the spider tongue of Mrs. Black in the main street. For you thought of Mrs. Black in terms of tongue, the rest of the body being merely scaffolding and machinery toward its proper functioning, the senses its vigilant feeders, and its unruly edge a living illustration of the truth in St. James's words. Gogol has a story about a man who met his own nose. It would be an appalling thought to imagine

Mrs. Black confronted with her own tongue, in the flesh, so to speak, and as her victims visualized it. On this particular evening, the tongue had nothing very definite to say, but nuance dripped from it.

"What a nice young man that new lodger of yours is, Mrs. McGough! And how reserved and quiet he is, too. Except, of course, when he is with that charming little girl of yours, Nell. Why, my dear, I saw them coming laughing and chatting together, and they did look a such sweet pair. Of course, there's nothing in it, for we all know where Nell's heart is, don't we? But they did look so sweet!"

Mrs. McGough hated this lady with good Christian hatred. Nothing sinful, of course—just that, in the case of Mrs. Black, she felt that the command to love one's neighbor needed careful and theological interpretation. She detested the sugared voice edging the politely barbed words simperingly handed out, like cakes at a garden party. Above all, her very soul revolted against the "nice" and the "sweet" and the "charming"—society burrs bristling in the native homespun of her language, as evidence of the fact that, some forty years ago, she had taken a post as governess and brushed the hem of high life. Her manner, her simper, her mincing words were the *noblesse oblige* which this entailed, and the result was good Irish gossip and slander served on a silver tray with a golden-party polish. She invariably stirred up foul depths of language in the subconscious of Mrs. McGough, but heroic restraint kept it in check. And she contented herself with a parody of the creamy smile and a magnificently satiric rendering of the sugared words. She did so, now, but went off muttering quietly under her breath some of the unpalatables that had forced their way up. One of them was an eloquent monosyllable which she murmured fervently five times like a prayer. It was meant as a summary of the lady, the simper, and the sugar.

Yet, the gossamer thread had been well and truly webbed about her, and a fly of discontent beat and buzzed in it. Come to think of it, just why were those flowers in the room? Why all the sweeping, dusting, and polishing, as if he were Solomon and the Queen of Sheba all in one? Why that extra shade of anxiety to have everything right on the table for his meal, which couldn't be written off as mere courtesy to a paying guest? Above all, why the pulsating anxiety, concealed well enough, it was true, yet revealing itself in the irritable mood and the curt answer, that night when he did not return until past midnight? The fly in the web continued to thrash about and to buzz many things in the ear of Mrs. McGough. By the time she reached the house, she was in anything but a "sweet" mood. And, just to improve matters for her, Nell was in the garden cutting flowers. The table was laid for her, and the kettle was beginning to sing. To relieve her feelings, she poked the fire viciously and noisily. The fire spoke her feelings for her in a few sizzling hot cinders dropped on the hearth. Then she stood looking out at Nell with a look that curved a few discontented question marks around the sprays of luscious roses that hung between her and the girl. That garden was Nell's pride and joy. Standing among the flowers, reaching

66

high for a full-blown rose, the unspoiled beauty of her face and the loveliness of her lissome body made her one with the riot of beauty about her. But her mother's eyes missed the beauty for the tangle of question marks that came between.

"And when might the bride be expected?" she asked the girl as she entered, ignoring the bright, "Hello, Mother," with which she had been greeted.

Nell laughed, but then she noticed the unsmiling eyes.

"Whatever do you mean, Mother?" she asked, and was annoyed to feel the pink flooding her cheeks.

"What's all the titivating of the pink room about?" she asked bluntly. "Things are sometimes said with flowers—an old-fashioned way, but sometimes useful still!"

"Oh, Mother," she remonstrated. "You know I put flowers in the sitting room and on the landing as well."

Mrs. McGough felt more irritated than ever.

"Maybe if you had a bit more to do, you'd have less time for frumpery and falas."

A pained and surprised look came into Nell's face, and the irritation ebbed quickly from her mother's. Nell McGough's industry was the admiration of the neighbors, and her mother knew she had said something just about absurd as it could be.

"Oh, I see," Nell answered quietly. "That thick scum on the water in the bucket that I forgot to empty is just where I was blowing bubbles, I suppose. It wouldn't be the dirt from the back kitchen floor and the cellar stairs, of course. And the dustpan I emptied wouldn't have been filled from the attic above, either, for, of course, I was playing house with it. And that heap of accounts on the table…"

"All right, all right, Nell, I'm sorry," she placated her. "I'm a bit tired and irritable and I heard some talk."

"Well, you might have used your 'a bit more to do' and your 'frumpery and falas' gibe to the face—it's not hard to guess whose it is—that sprouted the talk."

"All right, daughter, we'll leave it at that. I'm hasty with my words in the wrong places, sometimes, and God knows you work enough for six, and I would be swamped without you."

Meantime, the gossamer thread was wavering its way splendidly through the town and into the farm where John Boyd was working. It curled about him in a remark made by one of the men he had employed.

"I hear your girl is sweet on McCourt's new miller."

"What do you mean—sweet?" he answered aggressively.

"Oh, nothing, nothing," came the hasty answer. "It's just that you hear talk now and then."

"Talk! Talk! This place stinks with talk. If the Angel Gabriel came down and landed in the market square for just ten minutes, he wouldn't be able to fly back again for the muck they throw at his wings. 'Sweet,' is she, now? I know the simpering little stink of a mouth that does have that word in it—naming no names!"

"Ara, you shouldn't bother yourself about it," the other cut in anxiously. "Sure, talk is like the froth on a pint, just there to be blown away."

But John had already begun to bother—very much, indeed. He went morosely silent and remained as cantankerous as a broody hen for the rest of the working day. When the web of talk is effectively spun before a man's eyes, he begins to see everything through it and colored by it; he recalls things dismissed to be considered now in a new light; and, above all, he becomes injected with the virus of motive-hunting, the nagging and unceasing "why." He had refused to admit to himself that Nell had been cooling toward him; she had said she was tired, that there was an enormous amount of work to do in the house with the extra dinners for her father's laborers, and he had accepted that with relief. But now, one or two incidents came back to be reconsidered.

A few nights ago, he had held her in his arms in the shade at the end of the garden just inside the gate, as he always did when saying goodnight. Suddenly, the latch had rattled and she had pulled him quickly, almost frantically, into a deeper shade. The gate had opened to admit Murray, who passed up to the house without noticing them.

"We are shy, my pet," he had teased her.

"Yes," she laughed. "Why, I'm trembling all over."

She complained of a headache and said she had better get in and lie down. This had been sufficient explanation for the perfunctory kiss that met his eager lips. But now, seen through the web, it was all quite different. She had kissed him, he remembered, as someone would whose mind was entirely distracted by something else. He might just as well have pressed his lips against the bark of the tree beside them, for all the warmth there was in her response. He suddenly, found himself wondering whether it was altogether shyness that night, and whether it might not have been rather a conflict between two attachments in the girl's heart. She wants me, he mused, but he's not to see me with my arms around her. So that's it, is it! Other things began to be refocused to the new mood—rather frequent headaches lately, talk about there being so much to do in the house from a girl who couldn't be sated with work, little actions and omissions that were now seen as dodges and side-steppings. Boyd's nature had the simple, straightforward drive of the plow in it, and it went into a confusion of tangles when, now for the first time, he tried to grapple with something so complex as the crisscross of a girl's mind, where every line is like an emotional nerve. The whole thing bewildered and tired him. It was characteristic of him that he should make a clean, simple cut through it all.

There was a dance in Newry that night, and he had been offered two seats in a car that would take them there and back. About five o'clock, he called on Nell.

"What a pity!" she answered. "It's not two hours ago since I promised Mary Callaghan that I'd baby-sit for her tonight so that she and John could get to a picture."

He went straight to Callaghan's.

"Well, as a matter of fact," Mary answered his question, "it really doesn't matter whether we go or not, for I don't want to spoil such a good night on Nell. It was only the goodness of her heart that made her offer to come."

"She offered to come?" he repeated in amazement.

"Aye, surely, and what's the wonder in that? Sure the same lady would split her last halfpenny with you and then come after you, wanting you to take the farthing."

That was all very grand, he thought, but in the language he talked, the words "I promised" meant "I was asked." He went back to Nell. There was no point in making a scene—he hated scenes—so he contented himself with saying that he had met Mary and that she had said Nell needn't come. It did not occur to John that, again in the language he spoke, "I met" didn't mean "I went to see" nor did "needn't come" quite fit the facts. As always in such cross purposes, the motes were in the eyes of both parties. Nell consented to go, but without enthusiasm. He left her with a very troubled mind.

Maybe he was only imagining it all, for it seemed so impossible that Nell should act like that toward him. They had been children together: he had started her top, mended her skipping rope, taught her to play marbles, and got into a thundering row with her mother because she had worn away her thumbnail in the process. You still could see the slightest of scores on the nail, and they used to laugh over it together. The prime row, though, was on the day he pushed her too high on the swing, the rope broke, and she sailed gracefully through the air to land in a great soft cake of cow dung! He remembered especially her merry peal of laughter at the horror written on his face, and her sunny—"Don't mind. It'll wash off." They grew up together and all his companions had teased and envied him the good fortune of having the lovely

Nell McGough for his pal. With his first few shillings he got when he began work, he took her to Newry to the pictures, and they had fish and chips and ice cream afterward. He had felt like a king that night when she had slipped her arm through his in the street; and later, when he was leaving her home, she had murmured that he was very kind and very good to her, as she lifted her face to his with a strange, very happy expression. He had really kissed her then for the first time—not the kind of "sporty" kisses they had exchanged before, but a kiss that meant something and that said a whole lot. He remembered, with a smile, how she had suddenly got shy, had broken from him, and had run into the house.... It is doubtful if John ever heard those lines of Bridge's entitled: "I Will Not Let Thee Go," but if he had, he would have recognized his own *cri du ceour* at that moment. There were too many small, affectionate things, witnessed by sun and moon, that bound them to each other.

He had traveled a modest way on the road to success since that night when he entertained Nell out of his first small pay packet. Without allowing himself to become a skinflint, he had saved well and perseveringly, so that, when an uncle of his died leaving him a tidy bit of land in the neighborhood, he was able to stock it with the best machinery, and really get under way. His father had died some years earlier, and later on his sister married a Canadian and emigrated with him. An amazing bond of affection existed between his mother and Nell, and John had not the least qualm in planning to bring Nell into this house that had now virtually become his. He loved his mother, and he was glad that the bond between her and Nell allowed him to keep her in the center of his plans; but it was around Nell they really centered, and every thought and every plan got this meaning and its unity of purpose from her. Without her, his life would lack a sense of direction; with her, it had more than direction—it had positive drive. And now, with a heavy heart, he saw all this threatened.

He sat with her in the back of the car with his arm about her shoulders. She wore her shell-pink dance frock and, because she was so vague in her manner that night, it seemed to remind him all the more of the splendid dances they had had together, when her laugh would suddenly ring out to quicken the pulse of the hall and lighten the hearts there. Was this the same girl whom he remembered dancing in his arms a few weeks ago, her head thrown back, her face aglow with the sheer joy of life and movement, a smile on her face that made you think of the morning sun glistening on the dew? Tonight she was subdued, vague, and talked with a preciseness that revealed only too clearly the effort to keep her mind on the company.

Things were no better in the dance hall. The frequent question—"What's up with Nell ? She's very quiet"—put to him by many of his friends, set his nerves more and more on edge. She danced with an exasperating vagueness; and, to crown all it, she sat vaguely on through part of "Lady's Choice," until someone called her attention to him, sitting uncomfortable and red about the gills. She started, rose, and turned to him with a sudden spurt of her old vivacity which lifted his heart for a moment. But it did not last: before the dance was half over, she had lapsed into vagueness and was even dancing badly, an unheard of thing for gold-medalist Nell McGough. He knew, also, that a whisper had gone through the hall and there was some speculation centering around them as they danced, and many furtively inquisitive glances were cast at them. He was relieved when the last dance finished, for he had become thoroughly miserable.

In the spot where he usually said his goodnight, her lips met his with the same vague abstraction that had run like an irritating thread through the whole night; and suddenly he had quite enough. He took his arms from about her and stuck them deeply into his pockets.

"What on earth is wrong with you, Nell?" he asked sharply.

"Nothing, John. Sure, what would be wrong with me?" she asked.

"Look here, Nell, I'm not a fool. As far as any feeling or enthusiasm went, I might just as well have had the brush from your mother's kitchen with me. It couldn't have been more vague or less responsive."

"I'm sorry, John, but that's the way I felt."

"Nell, I came out tonight with the intention of formally asking you to marry me. Circumstances are not helping me, but maybe it is all the better, for in your present mood, you won't say anything through romantic intoxication."

He laughed with a hint of bitterness.

"John, please don't ask that now," she pleaded.

"I'm asking, Nell. I don't see what mood and moment have to do with answering a question like that. You either do want to be engaged or you don't!"

Like many another good man before him, John was behaving very idiotically indeed. They stood in silence for a few seconds. Nell's head was bent in misery.

"Well, that's my answer, I suppose," John said bitterly.

She was crying. She turned slowly and went up through the roses into the house. He watched her go, then he, too, turned and went quickly away, slamming the gate after him.

Two nights later, another gossamer thread curled its way through the town. Mr. McGough was returning from a friend's house in which he had already heard the bad news that fine, steady John Boyd had been taken home from a pub blind drunk. McGough knew why the lad was drinking, and he was bewildered and depressed about it all as he made his way down the street, for he loved John Boyd like the son it was not given him to have. Unfortunately for herself, Mrs. Black chose this moment to stop him.

"Good night, Mr. McGough," she simpered. "What dreadful news about that nice boy, John Boyd. Who'd have thought it of such a sweet, charming lad?"

"And how fortunate for you, dear, sweet, charming Mrs. Black," he snarled at her. "Since it gives you and your corner cronies another subject for your sniveling and your driveling and your slobbering and your old woman's cacking!"

"Oh, my goodness. You are being insulting…"

"Ara, go to hell," he cut in. "You'll find signposts guiding you there with 'nice' and 'charming' and 'sweet' written on them, and you'll find the roadside gutters running with saliva."

He walked away with long, purposeful strides. She stood looking after him, her mouth gaping. You could almost hear her thinking that the man had not been one bit "nice" to her.

CHAPTER THE SIXTH

Molloy's pub was one of those places that seem to hold their years in the dust that settles heavily on oak beams and skirting—a place toned to a brown consistency by a century of tobacco fog that has licked the walls, curled on the rafters, flirted with the lamps, wept on the window panes. To the left a door stood open on a little booth, so much in mood with the rest of the establishment that it might have been spun from the accumulated dust and memories of sixty years by those lazy spiders weaving on the rafters. In short, Molloy's was one of those places which are credited with having "character," where a Guinness is really good for you because it seems to slake your throat with a mellow, liquid wisdom— the wisdom of the clay and the crops.

Two men were sitting in the booth, facing each other across a small beer-stained table. The one facing the door sat slumped in his chair, his heavy, oozy flesh pushed up about him, so that he seemed to be grotesquely floating in a fleshy pool. There were years of lechery in those great, sagging globules of flesh; there was grossness in the face, cushioned in its oily succession of chins. The man sitting with his back to the door had a rather strange likeness to his companion, though perhaps likeness is scarcely the word. Rather would it seem as if, having a choice of somewhat similar material in two brothers, the soft and plushy vices had selected Luke and bloated him to their image and likeness, while the lean and hungry vices had stroked his brother into a tight-skinned, tight-tipped saw of a man, against whom no one could brush without being torn. When you looked into the eyes of these two men, you found little to choose between them but you selected Luke, for you saw the cold steel in the eyes of his brother. Two pints of Guinness stood on the table, and their creamy tops seemed the purest things in that company. One of the fleshy chins coagulated with the others, as Luke lifted his head slightly, took a long draw from his stout, scowled down at the new level thus occasioned, and darkened the scowl at his brother as though he, too, had sunk to a lower level in the process.

"So yeh won't lend me a lousy fiver, huh?" he grunted. "Your own brother, huh?"

With the last grunt he suddenly heaved himself upward and forward, seeming to drip his fat like a seal lifting itself out of mud, and sank back as suddenly, his flesh pooling about him.

"Yeah, I won't lend you a fiver. That's what I said," came the answer, slowly and callously casual, in a voice that had the hard lines of the man in it.

"Ah, have a heart, Patch," came in a kind of whine, "I'm down on my luck. I'll pay you back. I'll get a job. I'll…"

He was cut short by a hard brittle laugh.

"You'll get a job. So will my Aunt Fanny. Look, my bucko, the only job you ever got was the King's pleasure smashing stones. You'll…"

But the great hulk of flesh had risen, the face absurd with surprise, the eyes alive with astonishment, the mouth open, in a chaos of chins. Patch looked at him with amazement and then looked into the bar. What he saw there pulled taut the hard lines of his face in livid hatred, and his eyes became spitting points of steel. Hatred went out from him to the man who stood looking at Luke with a surprised, but clean and steady look. It was merely a matter of seconds, and the few standing at the bar scarcely noticed it. Murray turned to the bar, nodded to the men, bought some tobacco, and went out. A keen observer would have noticed a slight increase in the droop of the shoulders and a throbbing of a big vein in the forehead. Otherwise, there was nothing to show the moment of tense drama that had just occurred, except the drops of perspiration that suddenly gathered on the fat one's face as he sank again into the chair.

"You know that fellow?" Patch asked, leaning forward and speaking with a cold hate that seemed to lay each word flat on the table before his brother.

Luke started and looked sharply at him. The flat, level words reminded him of other things that could be laid flat on a table, and a certain cunning came into his eyes. It was his turn to be coolly smug.

"Maybe I do and maybe I don't," he answered carelessly.

"You'll tell me whether you do or not, or by heavens I'll…"

"Keep your hair on," Luke cut in sharply. "What do you want to know for, anyhow?"

Patch leaned forward and poured out a tale of wrongs done to him by the low cunning of this man, his hate feeding him with details and with a surprising eloquence. Brought up short by a sudden realization that he was talking to himself, he saw that the cunning was gone from his brother's eyes and that the fear had returned. Something he said had done this, and he cursed himself for it.

Luke seemed to come back from somewhere with a start.

"I'll not tell you anything about him," he said stubbornly. "I'll just give you one bit of advice. Keep away from him. There's something about that man…"

Patch felt the need for action. Diving into his pocket he fumbled for a second and then laid a five-pound note flat on the table, keeping his hand on it.

"Luke?" he said with slow significance.

Luke hesitated, but the fear in his eyes remained.

"Luke?" he said again, fumbling and adding a pound note.

"No, no, I won't!"

An answer meant a wavering, and Patch watched cupidity narrowing the fear-filled eyes.

"Luke?" he said, in a vibrant whisper, as he added two more notes to the pile.

The fear was gone from the eyes now, and a fat hand was already moving as though of its own accord toward the notes.

"Make it ten, Patch," he said.

More fumbling and more notes.

"Give me the money."

"And you'll tell me how you know that man and where you met him?"

"Yes, yes, yes," came the impatient answer.

Patch lifted his hand from the notes and Luke took them greedily. He counted and put them in his pocket.

"Hurry, damn you," his brother snapped.

"Well, if you must know, I met him in Dartmoor prison," he said, with a wry face as though each word tasted bitter.

"Ha!" Patch exclaimed, with an animal growl of satisfaction. "Not a jailer or anything?" he went on, with sudden anxiety.

"No a prisoner. In for some kind of jewel grabbing."

"You saw him there?"

"Yes," he answered, adding in a voice that trailed itself sullenly: "He was some months in already when I was jailed there."

Luke looked at his brother and was amazed at the fiendish satisfaction in his face at this disclosure. The fear was back in Luke's eyes, but Patch saw nothing, heard nothing, absorbed in his gloating, repulsive joy.

"Ha! Dartmoor! Jailbird! Holy St. Francis the second, a common jewel thief!"

"Patch," Luke's voice came in a whine, "leave him alone, Patch. I'm telling you. Don't say I didn't tell you. Don't blame me. I'm warning you."

"What the hell is wrong with you, with your sniveling and your trembling? Why should I leave the holy jailbird alone? I'll blast his halo for him and scatter its bits in the dung of the streets. Holy St. Francis of Dartmoor, my holy foot!"

Then a sudden idea struck Patch.

"Hey?" he said, "are you telling me everything? Meeting an old jug-pal doesn't scare you like that. Come on, now."

"No, I won't. I've said too much already. Leave him alone, Patch. That's all I'll say."

Again Patch's hand went fumbling into his pocket.

"There's twenty more where that ten came from, Luke."

"No, by heaven, not if there were a thousand and twenty."

Patch knew by the tone of his voice that it was useless to try again. Luke drained his stout in an unsteady, gulping draught, and stood looking down at the leer of satisfaction on his brother's face. Then he turned, and without another word, left the pub.

Patch continued to leer. He wondered what the secret was that Luke had kept from him. He had enough, however. Luke was telling the truth, and he knew that Murray did not lie. A plan had already begun to form in his mind.

The wind had risen and it was flinging great sheets of icy rain along the street. It stung cold on Luke's burning cheeks. Holding his coat about him, he battled his way into another pub, sat down heavily on a wooden seat by the counter and called for a double whisky. The sudden storm had made a thick twilight in the place, but the lamps had not been lighted. Luke gulped his whisky and cursed the half-light in which those ghosts of the past, that were already gibbering about him, could breathe and speak. They had risen, wraithlike, from the witches' caldron of his past, when he saw that face in the pub; he had mastered his fear, and had felt them sinking again as the bank notes spoke crisply under his fingers like words that break a spell; he had run from them, only to find their cold fingers feeling through the sleet for his face. A dark angel had descended into the hidden depths of him to stir the stagnant, pool of things resolutely forgotten. In the dim ocher of the room there were voices and visions.... The wraiths of a hundred better selves deliberately debauched rose from the slime in which he had crushed them. There were voices of angels and the clamor of demons—voices from those far-off years when he had, in the freshness of his morning, aspired to the heights of the priesthood. But they had rejected him. He had gone away dazed, yet with eyes still uplifted. The vision of the beckoning heights had faded, and bitterness had come on him moving slowly over his soul like a river of slime. He had fought that slime, but it had conquered him.

Yet there were times when his soul stirred under the slime and he cursed it violently; times when the vision of the heights had returned to trouble the mothy and warm sense twilight he had made for his breathing.... Slumped broodingly in that pub, he was again one of a sullen row of men walking across a prison quadrangle, the faces like bitterness made flesh. He had turned and looked into the eyes of the man who walked behind him, and he had quailed from what he saw there. They were the eyes of a good man, with light and peace and the secret of a great pain in their depths. He shrank from that secret; but he shrank, too, from the light and the peace. For Luke hated anything that made the trampled virtues stir in him. He cursed anything—look, word, prayer, memory—which served to crack the carefully laid soul slime and allowed the ancient beauty of the soul to shimmer ominously through.... Once, on the Thames embankment, a child, lost in watching a circling bird, had wandered to him and put her hand in his. He had felt a sudden softening in carefully hardened places, and he had flung the little hand from him. The eyes of that prisoner had done the same to him: he fixed his eyes avidly on the granite of the prison walls about him that its hardness might seep through him. But there was no comfort in that hardness, for when he turned from those eyes, he had taken their secret with him. But no, he mused, it could not be. Things like that happened only in books. He muttered to the prisoner in front—The tall one six behind, who is he? Don't know, came the furtive answer. In for jewel grabbing. Caught with the rocks, they say.... When Luke heard this, he became as a man who walks in his own hell. He could not escape from those eyes—from the light and the peace and the pain in them, from the secret in their depths. He hated the memories that meshed him like the flung threads of a torn design, half made in the image of a lovely thought, only to be ripped asunder in cynicism and revulsion.

Then had come the moment, when the sullen fires in the souls of chained men had flared into savage life, when knives had flashed in a moonlight riot, when a gun had spat and a clambering figure had dropped from the wall with a groan. A cold silence had followed, the last doubt of the prisoner's identity was removed for Luke, and in that full realization, he felt all that was good in him rising defiantly in the slime of his soul to spit the word "Judas" in his face. For the man of the dawn eyes had stepped forward suddenly. He had stooped over the huddled body of the shot prisoner and he appeared to be speaking with him. He continued speaking with him, even when an angry voice ordered him back, and a bullet ripped the stone a few feet above his head. Then he straightened and moved back, keeping his face toward the dying man. In that sulky silence of the beaten, Luke Rafferty had seen, had understood, and had covered his eyes from his fear standing before him. It was a horrible silence, a silence full of eyes, of eyes that had the soul-searching cleanness of the dawn in them....

Slumped on the seat of the pub, cowering, oblivious of everything, Luke Rafferty was again in the cold grip of his terror.

A great, horny hand, smelling of animals, was laid on his shoulder, and a voice came into his silence with a gruff kindness:

"You feeling bad? Why, if it isn't Luke Rafferty and no other. You were dozing and muttering something awful. Come and have a jug of Cassidy's consolation for the afflicted."

Luke looked up, dazed, and then he rose with a thirsty eagerness for the murk of smoke and chatter that would cloak him from the phantoms of his fear. The voice speaking to him was rich with reality, thick, solid, with the rumble of cartwheels and the slide of the soil in it.

"Ara, Luke, but aren't you the stranger about these parts, and no mistake about it! Sure, there's half of the men here wouldn't know you. Patch was saying you were holding down a very fine job as a secretary to something or other in London. I was never any good at brainwork. A bull for a book and a plow for a pen—that's me. Come on, what'll you have?"

They crowded about him, eager for news. Their talk was a soothing wall of sound about him, and Luke was soon himself again. He exchanged some stories with them, and his bellow of a laugh filled the room. So the night flowed on, pint following pint, until that moment of mellowness in which last drinks are called for. Suddenly, the door was shuffled open and an old, gnarled, twisted stump of a man came in crying that he had been robbed.

"The money's all gone. Every pound of it. God wither the hand that took it," he said bitterly, and the rest was lost in pitiful weeping.

But there was no need for any more. Every man there knew what "the money" meant, for the story of Old Tom's savings was part of the townland folklore. These savings—which he had kept hidden in his house, distrusting all banks—were to have saved the last rag of pride left to Old Tom. The house and the fistful of land would go to the sister's son, and the money would "bury me dacent," as he so often expressed it to his neighbors over a pint. There would be no pauper's funeral for Old Tom. No sir! The money was there, cozy and warm, the money for hearse and headstone, for priest and sacristan and server. And now, the money was gone.

Ten minutes later, Luke stood at the bottom of the deserted street, every globule of the heavy face sagged and sullen. In the gas lamp's soft light that was weaving a kind of crazy fabric through the drizzle into which the storm had abated, he looked at the notes in his hand.

"So, brother mine," he muttered, "you have sunk as low as that. You would even strip a corpse of its few rags of pride, curse you."

He hesitated, his lips quivering. Then he thrust the notes back into his pocket.

"And curse me with you. But I want the money."

He set off, walking toward Newry. His footsteps echoed among the wet and dripping trees that arched the road. They made a hollow, hammering sound. They were the footsteps of a man who was crucifying his soul on the wrong cross.

CHAPTER THE SEVENTH

Patch Rafferty was a hated and despised man. At the pitch-and-toss school where the four roads met, he was suspected of having slipped in the two-headed halfpenny with a greasy sleight of hand that beat the quickest eye. There is an old story about a visitor to Ireland who thought its religion was an open-air one of coins offered to the Deity, eyes raised to heaven and lowered to earth with exclamations that sounded like prayers. To develop the myth a little, it could be said that the two-headed halfpenny is the unforgivable blasphemy of this cult, the sinner completely losing caste. Patch had blasphemed, as everyone knew but no one could prove, and therefore his appearance anywhere near the crossroads was a signal for hostile silence and a gathering up of coins.

No man wanted a quarrel with Patch, for his revenge had the silence of the adder's tongue in it. Mick O'Neill had given him a clear summary of his character in a few words one night. Patch had gone white with rage and his eyes had spat. But he had made no threat nor struck a blow; he merely stood in a charged silence for a moment as though savoring and tasting the words, and went quietly away. They warned Mick, but he laughed at them. It would take more than that red bag of bones to do any harm. Two nights later, three ricks of O'Neill's were burned to the ground. Paraffin and a very cleverly arranged fuse had been reported, but there were no clues. One thing emerged in the police enquiry. The man who, according to alibi, seemed farthest away at the time was Patch Rafferty. A more recent piece of history was the poisoning of a valuable greyhound belonging to Farmer Daly, the very night he had occasioned Patch's downfall. It was a mysterious business, but, once more, the man on whom circumstantial suspicion fell least was Patch Rafferty.

Patch was feared as a snake would be; there was something low, cunning, silent, and slimy in him that never came into light but which was always there. Everything he did left a trail of slime: Patch Rafferty, his mark.

A social leper—and he knew it. When he came into a pub, the men ignored him, and he drank his stout and his whisky in sullen silence until the drink mounted in him and he fastened onto a group—talking, talking, talking. But no one would answer him. The campaign of silence had deepened in the few days past, for there were whisperings about the possible whereabouts of that money stolen from Old Tom. Nothing was said, of course, but there were cryptic remarks exchanged in a kind of impersonal tone about the man not being far to seek, the mystery not hard to clear up, and so forth. Anyhow, no one would risk having his health drunk in the price of a coffin and a shroud.

It is very unpleasant to play the role of a walking icicle freezing the atmosphere of a room, or to know your neighbors look for moral slug slime in the places you have been. Patch knew the temper of the town toward him, and reacted to it with silent fury. The moral opposite, in the contrast of black and white, to Patch, was the Stranger. The town made this very clear in the honor and respect with which they treated him.

Patch hated him in such a fashion that he regarded every respect shown to the Stranger as implied venom toward himself, because the Stranger had come to oust him. But there was more than a personal grudge in Patch; it was a question of two irreconcilable principles, two opposed philosophies of life, confronting each other in two men. It was of the nature of things that they should be so opposed, and that the hatred should be on one side only. Patch's hatred danced its triumph in his eyes as he left the public house in which he had spoken with Luke. He felt his grim secret like wine in his blood. It glowed in him, and he knew the pleasure of a secret cat-and-mouse play that was well suited to his twisted nature.

It was a pleasure that waited for him when he awoke the following morning. He made his way to the south road and stood in a corner formed by a gate and a hedge, which he knew Murray must pass on his way to the mill. It was easy for him to pass without seeing Patch, and on this morning he seemed so preoccupied that he scarcely seemed to see anything. Patch watched him pass. Then, when he had gone a few steps further, Patch stepped out on the road and gave a few derisive hoots after him:

"Straighten your halo, holy one," he jeered, "it may be slipping."

The Stranger stopped, half turned to Patch as if to say something, changed his mind, and went on with the same silent preoccupation.

Patch waited a few hours until the work at the mill was busiest. A row of carts stretched across the field, and the owners were loading them. Murray was moving along the carts with a ledger, making entries and totting figures. Patch moved along the line until he met the Stranger. He came up to him and laughed softly and obscenely in his face. Then he continued across the field. The Stranger watched him for a moment with very troubled eyes.

How much had Patch learned from his brother? This was the question which had torn the hours of sleep with the panic of two hands ripping a sheet. When, with great effort, he succeeded in dozing for a while, that question would rip across his sleep and wake him to a living fear. When the dawn came seeping through the curtains, and the pink walls began to show in the dusty half-light, he left his room, crept silently down the stairs, and was soon in the fields. He felt better for the coolness of the dew and the bravery in the bird songs. When you take your fear into the open with you, it does not seem to have the strangling nearness of four walls.

But for all that, he was unable to do more than play around with his breakfast. His throat seemed gritty and contracted, the food tasteless.

Patch's conduct left no doubt about the answer. Patch knew—how much, the Stranger could not guess, but sufficient to allow him the gloating pleasure of playing with a trapped victim. Sleeplessness, hunger, anxiety all combined to make him sick and dizzy; the figures on the ledger, like columns of ants, began to walk up and down and across the page. He stood for a moment, fingers pressed to his eyes; but it was hopeless. Finally, he called Tommy and told him he must carry on as best he could. He handed him the pen and ledger and retired into the mill. Alone, and suddenly very weary, he lay down on some sacks, one arm flung out, the other crooked under his head. In spite of the noise and bustle outside, he fell into a troubled sleep.

The door of the mill opened quietly and a ray of sun picked out the form of a young girl standing with a basket on her arm. It might have been a stage with the spotlight on her. She stood for a few seconds searching the gloom inside. Then, as her eyes became accustomed to it, she saw the figure lying on the sacks, like something flung down, lifeless. With a strangled cry, she rushed forward and went on her knees beside him. He was breathing heavily, his face half buried in the sacks. Wild with relief, she bent down impulsively and kissed his cheek. Then, suddenly overcome by what she had done, she sat back on her heels, buried her face in her hands, and began to cry. He stirred in his sleep, turned, and rose on his elbow.

Then he rubbed his eyes, came fully awake, and looked in amazement at the girl kneeling beside him, her face red with sobbing.

"It's Nell McGough, Michael," she said—it was only later that she would wonder at herself for using his Christian name—"I came with something for you to eat, as you made such a poor supper and breakfast, and then I saw you lying there like you were dead. And I'd rather be dead myself than that."

He looked at her in amazement and with a certain embarrassment for a moment. She had risen as she spoke, and now he pulled himself together and rose, too.

"You are very kind to me, Miss Nell," he said quietly, "but you must not allow yourself to feel more than kind."

As he spoke, she imagined she could see the redness of the flesh on his cheek where she had kissed him.

"I am not quite the kind of man you think me to be," he said slowly.

She looked at him silently for a moment. "I know you to be someone good, clean, and wholesome," she said quietly.

"Thank you for that," he answered. "Perhaps you may remember these words of yours at another time."

He stooped to the basket, took out the flask of tea, opened it, and drank deeply.

"This is, indeed, very welcome."

He escorted her to the door and again thanked her. Most of the carts had gone. She saw Tommy standing by one of them and she called out her goodbye. It was a great day for Tommy because he had really risen to the occasion and shown his worth.

On the way home, she wondered and wondered whether he knew she had kissed him.

It was two nights later and trade was at a peak in Cassidy's. Patch came in, and, as usual, the temperature dropped wherever he stood. He ordered a whisky, and putting his back to the counter he stood there, smiling smugly. Some of the men noticed the smile and wished they had the courage to step forward and wipe it off. It was insultingly smug and seemed a comment on the whole company.

"That fellow has somewhat up his sleeve," Big Bob Mullins said in an undertone to his group.

"Aye, he has that, and it's nothing good either."

Patch had taken a few whiskies now and was beginning to feel that his great moment had come. The smugness and gloating on his face had become repulsive.

"There are some people in this town," he said suddenly to no one in particular, "who'd like to be thought holy St. Francises, and are as crawling with maggots underneath as a sod you'd turn in your field."

Cassidy was immediately on the alert.

"Now, none of that in this house, or I'll…"

"Leave him be," Big Bob said, stepping forward. "Now, what was it you were saying?" he asked Patch with an ominous politeness.

The whisky was warm in Patch and he faced up to Bob.

"I was saying," he returned, with the same mocking

politeness, "that there are people in this town wearing a halo they have no right to."

"Name just one," Big Bob answered.

"Oh, that's not hard," Patch answered with a forced laugh. "You have only to go down to McGough's and you'll find him there. Murray's the name."

He looked around to see the effect of his words. The men looked at him for a few seconds of quiet contempt, and then little Tub Regan spoke for them:

"You're clean daft, man. Go away and see a horse doctor."

A burst of laughter greeted this and Patch's face flamed.

"Maybe I'm not as daft as all that," he snarled. "How many of you know that yon Murray is just an ex-jailbird fresh from Dartmoor?"

"Bats. Abso-blooming-lutely bats!" Regan commented.

But no one laughed this time. There was a dangerous look in Big Bob's eyes, when he said:

"Murray is a jailbird, eh?" he asked.

"Murray is a jailbird," Patch answered.

"Come on, men," he said, gripping Patch by the scruff of the neck and pushing him ahead. "I've been waiting a long time for this. You'll let your foul, lying mouth say those same words to the decent face of Michael Murray, and after that it won't be a horse doctor you'll be needing but the doctor they got for Humpty Dumpty."

They continued in silence. It took infinitely less than the strange sight of twenty silent men walking grimly behind Patch, to create a sensation in the little town. Doors were opened and curtains were drawn. A curious crowd joined the silent march, and many of the children ran from the houses telling each other that Patch Rafferty was going to be tarred and feathered at the crossroads. The group piled awkwardly into McGough's shop, and the last man closed the door to keep out the crowd. Mrs. McGough was in the shop, and, drawn by the sudden commotion, Mr. McGough and Nell were with her.

"What in heaven's name is all this?" she asked.

Big Bob stood turning his cap in his hands.

"It's Mr. Murray we'd like to see," he said grimly, with a significant side look at Patch.

Patch had had a few uneasy moments between the pub and here. Would Murray deny it? After all, perhaps Luke had been angling for the money, for his fear seemed too excessive to be caused merely by a reminder of jaildays. And besides all that, perhaps these men would give him a hiding, anyhow. The whisky had completely cooled in him by the time he reached the shop, and he felt a cold sweat break out on him when he heard Murray's footsteps on the stairs.

The little pink room was right at the back of the house, out of reach of the commotion in the street. Nell had merely called up to him that there was someone in the shop to see him. He was dumb with amazement when he saw the crowded shop, the grim, silent faces of the men turned toward him, and the cold hate in the face of Patch Rafferty who wasn't quite sure whether his role was to be that of a triumphant counsel for the prosecution, or of a cornered rat waiting to be kicked. For a second, Murray stood frozen, every drop of blood drained from his face. Then he stepped forward into the shop.

"You wanted to see me?" he asked in a tired voice.

"Yes," Big Bob said, stepping forward. "You must excuse us butting in like this, but this…this…"

A nudge of an elbow from Tub Regan and a whispered injunction made him curb his language.

"…this fellow here has made a filthy suggestion that we all know is wrong. But we want to hear you say it is, so that we can stuff it and his Adam's apple down his throat together. So, may we ask a question?"

"Certainly."

"Well, Mr. Murray, begging your pardon for even suggesting as much, were you ever in jail? I know the question is just plain daft and that the answer is no."

Murray turned quietly to Patch, whose avid eyes were fixed on him, and said quietly:

"The answer is…yes."

A gasp of astonishment greeted the admission. Patch became as a man transformed. The grin of smug satisfaction returned to his face and seemed like something he would wear to his grave as a man might wear a decoration of honor.

"You were in for jewel thieving?" Patch asked.

The Stranger stood silent for a few seconds.

"I was condemned for jewel thieving," he admitted in a voice that was very low and very tired.

The silence that followed was broken by hysterical

sobbing. Nell pushed past her mother, stamped her foot, and shouted:

"You weren't. You didn't. You know you didn't!"

Mrs. McGough came to life suddenly, and grabbed Nell by the arm. She pushed her into the kitchen saying:

"You catch yourself on, my lady. You've made a big enough fool of yourself already."

Her sobbing could be heard in the silence of the shop. Patch turned to leer at the men:

"Well, gentlemen," he said sarcastically, "who's to see the horse doctor now?"

He walked toward the door. His triumph was a barren one, for even in its greatest moment, they slunk from him as from a disease-slimed rat. They filed out quietly and dispersed.

The crowd outside was impatient for news. They had it served piping hot from Patch, who, reveling in the unusual experience of being a mob's hero of the minute, really let himself go.

"Now, who'd have believed it, and him going to the altar every blessed morning!"

"Shocking, isn't it? You don't know your own neighbors these days."

Such were the comments, more and more inane, until they reached the climax in the Widow Ryan's:

"If he had told us himself!"

She had, indeed, put her finger on the grievance of the mob—for mob it certainly had become, with all the irrationality of that Hydra-headed monster in every age and clime. He had offended against the unwritten law that everyone's business is the business of everyone else and that no man shall live in secret from his neighbors. He must now suffer for it. The word "jailbird" was bandied about. A little boy—one, too, who had received many kindnesses from the Stranger—now caught up in the excitement, climbed on the window sill, pressed his face to the glass until he could see the Stranger inside, and shouted:

"Got any diamonds, Mr. Jewel Thief?"

Murray knew the moment of Caesar when he saw Brutus's arm raised. He felt that the children, too, had turned against him, and that there was nothing more.

"I am sorry to have brought this on you," he said to Mrs. McGough.

She made no answer. Her face was set in the grim lines of the Pharisees when they saw the Magdalen. There was no hint of sympathy in the eyes. But the sobbing in the kitchen had not ceased.

The taunt of the child had released something in the worst elements of the mob. A stone struck the window, the glass quivered, then sprinkled in fragments on the floor. A few viciously pointed sabers of glass, precariously loose, were all that remained.

As he climbed the stairs, he heard angry words between Mrs. McGough and her daughter. One sentence came clearly to him, one of those sentences whose symbol is the cloth with which the Face was wiped on The Way. Nell had said:

"He is good, fine, noble. I'm sick of being told he said it himself. I'm sure we're all wrong somewhere."

The crowd has dispersed, the main body returning toward the center of the town. At the corner of one street, a woman, wild eyed, her shawl slung on carelessly, her white hair streaming in the wind like a maenad, met them, and stood in their way. She lifted her arms and began to shout at them. They recognized her as the Widow Muldoon, a woman whom every person there respected as the bravest fighter of adversity in the whole parish. A sudden hush came over them, and a sudden awe. For here was a woman, a "good, dacent woman," suddenly coming forward as a denouncing prophetess. Her voice rang clear in the night air, and every word had the lash of a whip in it.

"See the conquering heroes come. Aye, you are a great lot! Out jewel thief hunting—the latest sport of the parish! But I'll tell you something. Who was it, Johnny McCabe there, who clothed your two youngsters for Confirmation when you hadn't a halfpenny to jingle on a tombstone? Aye, and don't blow a trumpet about it either, like some folks here if they put a halfpenny more than twopence by accident in the poor box.

"And you, Billy Madden, you mind the time the cobbler Casey said not to bother paying for the repairs of the youngster's boots. Ever ask yourself why? Casey's a careful Christian and knows the color of his money. And I'm here to tell you something. Who did you think sent my Kathleen to a sanatorium and is paying every halfpenny for her there?"

Silence followed, for they were very impressed. Then a voice said:

"Aye, and where did he get the money to do it?"

"I wouldn't doubt you, Paddy Boyle," she blazed, "for you'd suspect your own mother. Now, where's the breed of jewel thieves who came along looking to spend their money on charity. Have a bit of wit, man!"

No one else attempted to answer her. The disintegration of a mob does not take long, and when men become individuals again they scarcely recognize their mob selves. Individual values emerge, memories are awakened, consciences are pricked. Reaction shows itself in a desire to creep away and hide in a corner. It had already set in with these people, and they were glad to escape from the lash of Mrs. Muldoon's tongue.

She pushed her way through them and went on to McGough's. Mr. McGough met her.

"Do you honestly believe that this man is a criminal?" she asked.

"Well, he says himself..." he began hesitantly.

"Answer my question, Jimmy McGough, or aren't you man enough?" she interrupted.

"Heavens, Brigid, but it's yourself is fair roused this night. Well, to tell you the truth, I don't."

"Aye, and you're right. The man that's spending his money on my Kathleen is no thief or common jailbird."

Mrs. Muldoon was not the only one who thought the circumstances had freed her from her promise of secrecy.

There were others. Things began to be whispered—things that had been double-cloaked with a promise of secrecy and with the curtain of a poor man's pride. Before the night was over, it was generally felt that the town had made a fool of itself. The mood of the following morning would not be healthy for Patch Rafferty, hero of a hectic minute.

CHAPTER THE EIGHTH

The Stranger was glad to reach his room, for at every step he seemed to be lifting leaden weights. He sat down heavily on the bed and buried his face in his hands. A great numbness like a thickening of his blood deadened him, and his mind seemed to be swimming away from him, through regions of sunshine and gladness, through tunnels of gloom and despondency never entirely unvisited by hope.

It was again the morning of his ordination. Sunshine colored by the stained glass, seemed to lay light-woven vestments in the aisle before the feet of those who were now lovely with the priesthood of Christ. He had thought of how they had "laid their garments before Him," and the bright reds and purples on which the procession walked might well have been angelic garments laid down in wonder and in awe of something that was not given to angels. The organ was playing Aquinas's *Panis Angelicus*—Bread of angels become the Bread of men, and yet the awful power not given to angels but to the clay hands of men. He lifted his eyes to where his family knelt, and he saw his mother's face. She appeared transfigured, and great tears were wet on her cheeks—tears that had a rapture in them, tears that were the tears of many sorrows radiant with blinding joy. A strange thought occurred to him just then. There was a certain moment in the Mass he would celebrate next morning, when a few drops of water, symbol of humanity, would be added to the wine, symbol of Divinity, and he would pray that as the Godhead took flesh, so also flesh might become as God. How lovely it would be if he could gather those tears of his mother, and let them fall—drop, drop—into the chalice of his first Mass. He could not do so, of course—it was just a lovely fancy— but he knew that Christ would see those tears in the drops which leavened, as with humanity, the Divinity hidden in the appearance of the wine.

Outside, the sunshine dazzled him after the cool shadow of the college chapel, but he knew that he had now within him something splendid, that owed nothing of its white effulgence to the sun. The priestly power seemed like something tangible which he held in blessing over the heads of the people that its radiance might be on them. The dust of the years might dim that radiance, the commonplace might lay its clogging chains on the swiftness of first rapture, but for that moment the priesthood was a great, gleaming sword of the spirit, mystic, wonderful.... He remembered the tear-wet face of his mother when she knelt to kiss his hands....

And then he remembered that face, as he had never seen it, save in his troubled dreams, bewildered, ashamed, lined with a dry sorrow that wouldn't soften in tears....

His first mission—a London slum, where his flock comprised the descendants of those who had fled from hunger in Ireland to filth and vermin abroad. Man is half a god and half a beast; but if you bury him in filth, the god wilts in him and the beast rises. Father Michael Murray met the challenge of a tired faith with all the energy of his priesthood. He worked, prayed, organized, kept interminable appointments with borough officials who came to him trailing tangles of red tape, with a horde of forms, BX this and AC that, whirling like dead leaves about their feet. He argued, pleaded that something might be done for his people; but each time he received another form, of another color, of another letter, of another number. Meantime, nothing was done, and the stench of the ill-ventilated, insanitary tenements continued to be the home of those who, as he tried vainly to convince them, bore the breathless tide of sons of God. They just laughed at him, pointed to their sty, and told him that their real tide should be that of pigs. Sometimes they spoke to him of Karl Marx, the man whose followers would deliver them from the mud. When the priest told the officials of this, they became yet more smug and complacent, smiling at him as one smiles tolerantly at a persistent but rather amiable child. Like many a zealous priest before him, Father Murray's health broke down under the strain.

His bishop had directed him to take a complete rest in the good air of Brighton, and had booked a room for him in the Marisma, one of the biggest hotels there and one in which His Lordship was sure the food and attendance would be good. He had already spent a week there and was feeling something of his old energy returning to him.

On Sunday night a storm had arisen. Great masses of water were lifting themselves like rearing horses, standing gracefully for a second, their crests like manes, then crashing in a chaos of foam. The moon had come out from a scurry of clouds and was casting a troubled, heaving path of silver on the sea. Father Murray stood at his window, entranced with the beauty of it all. A dance was in progress downstairs, and the entire hotel seemed to have emptied itself down to it. Now and then the music reached him faintly in little eddies of rhythm. Standing there, he had the pleasant feeling of having the whole place to himself. So filled was he with the beauty of the storm that he did not hear certain furtive fumblings at a door some rooms from his own, nor the quiet shutting of the same door a short time later. Quiet footsteps on the corridor and a quiet knock at the door. At first, he thought he had only imagined it, but the knock came again.

A great hulk of a man stood in the light of the opened door.

"Pardon my intruding," he said, "but you are a Catholic priest, aren't you?"

"Yes, I am a Catholic priest."

"Have you faculties to hear confession in this place? I have great need of the Sacrament and I won't have a chance of receiving it again for a long time."

"Come in," the priest had said.

Sitting heavily on the bed, his face buried in his hands, the Stranger saw that scene as if it were being enacted again in the little pink room of McGough's that had been, until half an hour ago, a haven of peace for him. He saw the man move across and kneel down beside the chair, his back to the window. He saw the face clearly, the face that was to meet him again in Dartmoor, the face that saw him in Molloy's and quivered with fear, the face of Luke Rafferty. It must have been when he turned to the wardrobe to get his stole that he missed his visitor's quick movement—a movement by which something was pushed into a ridge of woodwork under the seat of the chair. Whisky fumes rose like incense from the hulk of kneeling flesh, and for a moment he had had his doubts as to the propriety of hearing his confession. He spoke with him for a moment, but the man seemed impatient to be absolved. He seemed coherent enough.

"I have been a clerical student," he said, "and you know the old saying of the corruption of the best being the worst. But I am tired of it. Tonight, I have stolen much money and many valuables. But I suddenly felt a wave of self-disgust come over me, that I had sunk to the level of a common thief. I thought of you, and a great desire for the old cleanness possessed me. I suddenly wanted a clean incision that would rid my soul of the filth of many years. So I left my booty in a safe place in the lobby at the foot of the stairs where they are sure to find it."

He heard his confession, gave him absolution, and in a few moments he was gone. It had all happened so suddenly that he felt quite bewildered as he settled himself in his chair to finish the reading of his Office. He read on for half an hour. It had grown late and the movements and laughter of the returning dancers reached him from the corridor. Suddenly there was a startled shout and an excited babble of voices. Thinking his help might be needed, he opened the door and looked for a moment toward the group. Some of them turned and looked at him, something was said, others turned and looked. He went back into his room and closed the door.

Each night he liked to walk a little, whatever the weather and however late the hour, for it helped him to sleep. It was loss of sleep, more than anything else, that had undermined his health. The night was stormy but not wet, and the good breeze would whip the old energy back into him. He buttoned his overcoat, settled his hat firmly, and had his hand on the door when it opened to admit the proprietor, a detective, and a very distraught woman.

"Excuse me, sir," the proprietor said, "for coming in like this. There has been a serious theft and we are holding a routine check…"

Even with the great, obliterating stretch of years between, the Stranger could again feel the coldness that went through him at these words.

"Please do so," he said quietly.

They were making a thorough search. In lifting his chair, the detective tilted it, and a packet fell out on the floor. It burst, to reveal an ornament studded with jewels. With an excited cry the woman leaped forward, seized it, and held it to her heart as if it were a reprieve from death. The situation had become very complicated for him suddenly, for he was just a young priest unused to complexities. Without thinking, he said:

"The rest, then, will be safe at the foot of the stairs."

It was only when he had said this that the full horror of his situation came to him like a stunning blow. All his information was matter revealed to him in confession and was therefore sealed with the secrecy of the Sacrament. He saw sudden suspicion and hostility in the eyes that watched him, and he felt that a great desert of silence lay between them and him. A terrible injunction, the voice of his priesthood in him, imperatively commanded silence. Every circumstance pointed an accusing finger at him: the jewelry hidden in his chair; the fact that he had been alone on the floor of the hotel; his knowledge of there having been other booty which—of course—was not in the place he had said; finally, his apparent readiness to make a getaway. The detective stepped forward and said:

"I'm afraid I must ask you to come with me, and I must warn you that anything you may say may be used in evidence."

"I have nothing to say," he answered in a tired voice.

They left the room together and the crowd outside the door formed a gaping guard of honor for them. He heard some whispering—"It was a Catholic priest did it." "Fancy that, dear, a Roman clergyman"—those phrases that would come to full stature in the heavy glaring headlines of certain papers in Armagh, Derry, and Belfast, which—forgetting the good old Fleet Street axiom that only man bites dog is news—dearly love a Romish scandal. He thought of his mother's eyes resting on such headlines, and he felt his whole soul crouching as from a blow. On the fringe of the crowd in the corridor stood Luke Rafferty, asking what it was all about and making it obvious that he had just come in. The priest would have liked to look at him as he passed, but even this was forbidden him. The great priestly command to keep silence extended even to the least gesture. With downcast eyes and grim face he walked silently before the detective.

In the courthouse it was the same: a great silence hung between him and his accusers like a curtain of glass which allowed him to see them, but through which he could not speak or make a sign. He stood undefended, for he had refused the offer of counsel. His bishop had visited him, had arranged for bail, had spoken with him, and had finally turned away in despair from the stolidity that seemed suddenly to have possessed this so lately intelligent priest. Perhaps, His Lordship thought, the recent sickness had produced a kind of permanent manic depression. Perhaps it was one of those rare, very strange cases of unorthodox seeking for the confessor's halo. Perhaps…but what was the use of guessing, for everything was met with an infinitely respectful, pained, and bewildered silence. Everything possible had been done, and in spite of this, the priest now stood in the dock as a man who wears silence like a garment.

In a crowded court, the charge was read, and the question—Guilty or Not Guilty—died, syllable by syllable, in the silence. There was a moment's pause. Then the prisoner spoke in a clear and steady voice:

"My Lord, may I ask a question?"

"You may," came the answer.

"Thank you, My Lord. My question concerns the precise nature of the answer I am supposed to give. Is this answer purely a legal fiction?"

"Yes," the judge answered, somewhat puzzled. "It has no juridical force. It is splendid," he added, with that dry, inappropriate humor in which judges take an almost sadistic pleasure at times like this—"It is splendid to notice such a nicety of conscience in the prisoner at the bar."

The remark was rewarded with the usual amused rumble. But the prisoner did not smile. He whispered a weary "not guilty," which barely reached the ears of judge and jury, and then lapsed into silence as though the subsequent proceedings had no further interest for him. The jury brought in a verdict of guilty and the judge sentenced him to three years with hard labor. Very soon afterward, when his bishop had deprived him of all his priestly privileges, the numbness of his soul was complete.... And it was a gala day for certain papers in Armagh, in Derry, in Belfast. The God of Battles—particularly of the Battle called Boyne—had raised the veil a little on the secret iniquities of the Scarlet Woman of Babylon.

Bitterness came to him in his cell—a bitterness that settled like caked mud on his tongue and would not let him pray. All the things he had dreamed of, the things he had shaped in the image of his prayer, had ended in this bankruptcy of disgrace. He thought of his mother, of her bitter sorrow in the evening silence of the home he loved, with only the relentless ticking of the clock for company. The fire on the hearth would leap into life when she threw more wood on it, and the light would dance on that great picture of himself as taken on his ordination morning. Perhaps she was even then looking at it. Or, perhaps, some well-meaning neighbors had come to sit with her, and she was bravely trying to talk. It would soon be getting dark and they would leave her. Then she would stand at the back window, looking wistfully at the old mill where his father, God rest him, had lived and worked. He had worked with his father, but the call to the altar had been too insistent. The crop he was to mill would not grow in earthly soil. In the dusk, the old mill would be dim, like a memory of itself; there would be other memories, too, crowding that kitchen, and they would be draped in the shadow of sorrow. There would be some quiet whisperings where the men met in the dusk at the crossroads, but there would be a great sadness in the whispering; for on the infinitely rare occasion when a priest "goes wrong" in Ireland, a veil of silence, wet with the tears of her people and heavy with their prayer, is quickly drawn over the deed. It is "a fearsome thing," almost as though God Himself had erred.

"But for me," wrote Oscar Wilde when he penned his *De Profundis* in the dimness of his cell and in bitterness of soul—"But for me the world is shrivelled to a handsbreadth, and everywhere I turn, my name is written on the rocks in lead." When the clang of the door and the echo of the warder's feet had died away, Father Michael Murray knew that same feeling of a narrowed and narrowing world where the air was full of accusing voices and thronged with fingers that pointed their scorn at him, that wrote his name everywhere in the dust of his shattered world, or silently and steadily pointed at the priesthood he had besmirched. Wilde could see his grief as the red gore that ended a primrose path of vice. "There was no pleasure I did not experience. I threw the pearl of my soul into a cup of wine. I went down the primrose path to the sound of flutes. I lived on honeycomb...." The wine into which Michael Murray, in the freshness of his youth, had cast the pearl of his soul was the Wine that is the Blood of God. His path had been the hard one of moral and intellectual self-discipline, the rugged path to the beckoning heights. And it had all ended in dryness and shadow.

For the sorrow that filled the soul of Father Michael Murray was not the bitter dregs of jaded vice: the shadow that darkened on him had the mystery of Calvary in it—a shadow shared by a dying God. He had settled into the hard routine of daily work and his consecrated hands were becoming hard and calloused. He watched them dry and harden and crack as if they were an image of his own soul. The priest who came to minister to him found him always eager to receive the Sacraments, yet always quiet and almost morose. But the Sacraments have a mighty power of their own, to work beneath the crust of earth's sorrows, and suddenly to burst that crust as with a river of light. Theologians call it "the gift of sensible devotion"; it is the moment when parched but faithful lips know the caress of the cooling waters. It may be for only a moment, but the desert is never so dry afterward because the sky has become kindly with the softness of resignation.

The visiting priest had left him some books. Among them was a slim volume by François Mauriac called *God and Mammon*. He had begun to read it listlessly, but its beauty and sincerity very soon gripped him. It was a hot summer's night and the last birds had ceased to sing. He was glad of that, because there is no lift in the song of a bird heard in a prison cell, for it comes thronged with memories. He remembered a poem he once learned:

> *A linnet that had lost her way*
> *Sat on a blackened bough in Hell,*
> *Till all the souls remembered well*
> *The trees, the wind, the golden day.*

Yes, and the whiteness of a Host raised for adoration, the joy of hands raised in absolution. He did not like his cell to be peopled with the phantoms of memory, and he had turned from them to Mauriac's pages. He was soon engrossed in them and night was beginning to drape his cell with shadow. Unable to tear himself from his reading, he tilted the book to catch the last rays of light that now but faintly veined the gathering darkness. The words seared his brain with their beauty and he read them in breathless wonder:

> We are born the prisoner of our cross. Nothing can tear us from it. But it is peculiar to the Christians of my country to believe that they can come down from their cross. And in fact they do come down from it. Thus much are they free: they can refuse the cross. They go away from it, lose awareness of the mysterious thread which binds them to it and which they stretch so excessively that if ever they turn back they can no longer see the fatal sign in the sky. They go on and on until, stopped by an obstacle and suffering from a wound in the heart, they stumble and give in. Then, however utterly they may have been lost, once again the bonds draw them back with a surprising force, and once again they are mercifully hurled against the wood. As by instinct they stretch out their arms and offer their hands and feet, already pierced from childhood.

"*Mercifully hurled…*" The words seemed to hang in letters of sound on the air for a moment, and then suddenly to fill his cell as with the clash of cymbals. His whole soul rose to their splendid paradox with an exaltation that was very near to ecstasy. He—Father Michael Murray—had been, in the strange designs of God, "mercifully hurled against the wood." His path was wet with the blood of his pain; his dusty hours were filled with the dull sound of the crucifying hammer. And yet, in a blinding flash, it was given to look into the mystery of it all; to see that, in a world that was "living and partly living," he had been chosen to underline, with a red line written in the pain of life, the mystery of a mighty truth. Intoxicated with his thoughts, he lifted his arms and stood for a few enraptured seconds in the posture of one who is crucified. Then his arms sank slowly and he went on his knees by his hard cell bed.

The following morning brought its grayness and made its dusty answer to the ecstasy of the night shadows. But the moment of exaltation had not visited him in vain. It had not removed the sorrow from those eyes, but it had left in them a courage and resignation, that had the coolness of deep waters.

It was this quality of calm, resigned sorrow, mingled with priestly dignity standing erect before the tribunal of conscience, that awed Luke Rafferty in the morning parade of sunken men. But it was the charity of Christ in the eyes from which he slunk. It was those same qualities, meeting him as a strange, unfathomable thing, that numbed the raised arm of his brother Patch, and prevented a sacrilegious blow.... It was those same depths that lured the heart of Nell McGough, and made her blunder into believing that they craved for human love.

Night had come on him, flowing like a river of darkness through the rent in his soul: lonely stretches of desolation lay before the eyes of his soul, and he sat before his desolation, holding the cold body of his dreams in his arms, as

Mary had held her Son. But his comparison was a whip of light cutting across his sorrow. The thought of Mary can be as a drop of rich wine dropped into the brine of our sorrows to suffuse it as with the blood that filled the veins of God. In the few minutes before he reached for the book that contained the magnificent phrase: "mercifully hurled against the wood"—needle of light to pierce his brain—a strange warmth, a confused vision, had filled his soul. Later he would remember it as the warm light that surrounds the thought of the Mother of God, and when, later, he met those glowing words of Bernanos—a writer whose mind is as a splintered mirror held up to the angels, catching blinding flashes of their intuitive light—he would find in them the key to his confused visions and he would copy them out in a hand that shook in excitement and joy. For Bernanos would tell him of "the sublime being whose tiny hands hushed the thunder, hands full of grace—I watched her hands. I kept seeing them and not seeing them, and as the pain surged up in me and I felt myself reeling again, I caught one of those hands in mine. It was a child's hand—a child of the poor—rough already from the washtub.... And it was the face of a child, too—or a very young girl—only without the spark of youth. It seemed the very face of grief, but of a grief I had never known, which I could in no way share. It was so near to my heart, the wretched heart of a man. There is no human sorrow lacking bitterness, but this sweet sorrow lacked even strife—it was only surrender. It made me think of a vast soft night...."

The little bed in McGough's back room had become again the prison pallet; the room had taken on the gray grimness of a cell; the crouched man, burning face buried deep in his hands, was again the gray battlefield of despair and hope. Then, he had been "mercifully hurled against the wood," but a vast softness of a night, whose stars were the path of a Queen, had come about him, soothingly, and a voice had spoken the word of surrender in the warm blackness. That word had lived with him through his dragging years of prison gloom; it had walked with him through the gate on the morning they had released him. And he had crept back to the world, anxious only to remain a nameless shadow in the warm darkness breathing and breathed on by resignation. But now, the word had deserted him and his soul was dry as the floor of hell. For hell must be like that—a weird and pathless state of soul, a loveless bitterness, hands that reach out for the waters of love and find nothing in them but a dry sand that tortures the dry lips. A dry torpor had come on him; it was as though the green pasture about him had been blasted with a curse, and, in mockery of the Psalmist, his soul had crouched to feed on grit and sand....

When he lifted his head, silence had settled heavily on the house. There was no movement. He wondered what time it was, but his watch had stopped. The night had settled into heavy rain, and the wind had risen to fling it fitfully in great handfuls against the window panes. Fever burned in his blood and mounted to his brain. He struggled to his feet and made his way blindly to the window. Hungrily, he pressed his forehead to the cold panes and they were like cool, caressing hands. But the blackness outside held the lines of his despair, and it seemed one with the darkness that held him. Suddenly, a tumult of thoughts was in his fevered brain, caught and tossed and flung as the wind was doing with the great steady sheets of rain outside. The darkness was kind, the darkness was nameless, formless; you could be unknown in the darkness; you could take your secret with you and leave the people for whom you had become a scandal and a stumbling block; go, go, go, the darkness is soft, and the peace you seek is in its heart. He stumbled back to the bed, but the fever had risen in him like a boiling sea, and the air was full of urgent voices goading him. He rose quickly, removed his breviary from its carefully locked hiding place, pushed it into his pocket, buttoned his raincoat to the neck, pulled down his hat firmly, and a moment later he was quietly closing the back door of the house that bore the name McGough, the tipsy G now swaying gaily in the wind. It was hard to shut the door against the careering wind. Icy sheets of rain raced across the field, slapping against him. But he only noticed them as something which soothed the fever raging in his blood.

Inside the little pink room it was now quiet, save for the hit and wash of the rain on the window, the moan of the wind, and a steady dripping sound on the floor under the window. He had upset the vase of flowers, arranged with such care. The flowers lay huddled in a damp mass, and the water was dropping to the floor. It made a hollow sound in the room, like a cruel word mercilessly repeated.

CHAPTER THE NINTH

When Brigid Muldoon had turned from him, her eyes flaming, her long, white hair hanging like unraveled ropes about her face, Jimmy McGough stood on his doorstep like a man who has just been struck. He had been at school with Brigid, and he remembered the beauty of her thick golden hair and the deep calm of her blue eyes as she sat among the girls. There were other eyes among the boys that strayed often in her direction: but, when Michael John Muldoon, some years later, began to woo her, they all held back, for which of them would dare to match his own freckled lumpiness against the fine figure, face, and wavy hair of the fastest forward on the local team? Anyhow, when they saw the flushed, excited face of Brigid on the side line, following his every move, and her interest ebbing when the ball was not near him, there was no doubt as to how the cat had jumped. Jimmy had seen that flushed and excited face again, still strangely beautiful in spite of the thorny years into which fate had flung her—death, sickness, disappointments, the weary and wearing struggle to make ends meet.

But it was her eyes that kept him on the doorstep for a few pensive moments. Beautiful eyes never lose their beauty; they have been called the windows of the soul, and perhaps the inability of the blows of life to mar them is meant to underline the superiority of the soul. Beautiful eyes change their beauty; the lift and flash of youth sobers into the calm of middle age, and this calm takes on a deep, autumnal quality with the ripening of old age. Brigid's were at the stage of calm, but he had just seen it stirred up in indignation—and in indignation against *him*, Jimmy McGough. He could not bear that Brigid should think little of him, and her words—"Answer my question, Jimmy McGough, or aren't you man enough?"—had gone through him like a knife.

Was he man enough? Why didn't he step forward, as his good sense bade him, and stand in with Nell when she shouted this man's innocence in all their faces? A peace-at-most-prices man, he had allowed his personality and initiative to be swallowed up in those of his wife. What she said went, and the result was peace. But the result was also a bleaching of his own personality. He had taken to drink rather heavily for a while, but had tightened himself up in time. She took the credit for that, though she magnanimously shared it with one or other—he could never remember which—of the saints that hung in all corners of the house, making it look like a kind of portrait gallery of the kingdom of heaven. Sometimes he thought that if any of these revisited the earth and glided into McGough's, they might be anything but flattered at the confections that piety had made of them. But the immediate result of his reform was an even more effective bleaching, for he discovered that he had become one of those "poor men" who were "now keeping straight, thanks be to God." He had no objection to God being thanked, but being a subject for constant gratitude can be a bit wearing on a man. Mary was a darling and a good wife to him, but she could be a bit trying at times.

All this tumbled itself through his mind as he stood for a few seconds on the doorstep—wild horses released in him through a flick from Brigid's tongue. He was suddenly tired of it all. Perhaps he had got his peace at too big a price. He had not dared to mention John Boyd's name in the house since Nell's break with him, much less ask her what the stupidity was about. He missed John's cheery company and the merry laugh which he thought fitted so well with Nell's own silvery ripple. He didn't ask because if there was one fixed idea in Jimmy McGough's mind that pope or bishop couldn't dislodge, it was that women can't think. When you reason with them you get nothing but heat and emotional outpourings, and to bring a man's reasoning between two women is like trying to settle an argument between two blast furnaces by holding an icicle between them. This was what he thought, anyhow, as stepping into the hall, he paused to hear the raised voices from the kitchen.

"He's getting out of the house, bag and baggage, tomorrow morning. I won't have my business ruined by having a man like him in my house!"

(I wouldn't doubt you, Mary, he thought, for the money has coppered you a bit.)

"Why must he, Mother?" Nell sobbed. "I know he's kind and good, and just couldn't be what they say he is."

"How do you know, my knowledgeable Miss? You know so much about men that you hadn't the wit to keep a good one when you had him because there was another with some kind of fancy secret. Secret. I'll secret him."

This was the first open reference to the storm in the family teacup, and Jimmy leaned forward to catch what Nell answered in a low, calm voice.

"John was not such a good one with you, till his uncle's will made him a bird worth lifting off the bush. I think I vaguely remember that he was once 'a fancy, penniless scut,' and that it was someone else who was the fine, upstanding lad. Oh, Mother, do be fair."

Jimmy grinned in the darkness. Mary had certainly got her answer, and Nell's spirit must certainly be rearing when she dared to answer her mother like that. Though Jimmy had no respect for a woman's reasoning, he had every respect for her intuition—especially when that intuition was Nell's. That Nell should take up this firm stand in defense of the Stranger was more convincing to him than the verdict of a jury. Besides, what she had just said about John might be the prelude to better things.

He opened the door and stepped into the silence that Nell's words had created. Her mother was standing looking at her, a flabbergasted expression on her face. He ignored them both, sat down at the fire, and buried himself in the evening sports news.

"Your father should have come a few seconds earlier to hear that speech of yours, my lady!"

"Have you been cheeky to your mother? Repeat what you said."

Nell looked at him with the clear, level glance he loved in her.

"I merely said that Mother did not consider John Boyd such a suitable match for me till a farm changed the M into a C and the match into a catch!"

"I don't think you put it quite so pertly, Nell," he said, "if the few words I heard as I came in are any indication. But," he added, looking at his wife, "she needn't remember that for her next confession, because that, if I remember correctly, would come under the heading of Home Truths."

It was more than an answer—it was a vindication, a flush of color through a bleached personality, a beginning bravely made. Nobody, Brigid Muldoon nor anyone else, would get another opening to ask him was he a man or a mouse. He had squeaked long enough in the interests of peace, anyhow.

Mrs. McGough sent shafts of amazement and hurt feelings at him, but he had retired behind his paper.

"Well, all I can say is that this house is going mad!" she stormed.

The angry splashing of a jet of hot water from the scullery tap, turned full and viciously on, soothed her a little. Jimmy continued to smoke with aggravating calm, secretly savoring his first victory for years. Nell had taken up some knitting of hers that had lain neglected for days. She must, indeed, be very confused in mind, Jimmy thought, to continue a pull-over she had started for John Boyd. She knitted on for a while, and then seemed suddenly to come alive to the irony of what she was doing. She went scarlet, laid it quickly aside, and picked up a book. Her father watched her out of the corner of the eye. Five minutes went by and she had not turned a page. Then, with a little sigh, she laid the book down and picked up the knitting. That's right, my girl, he thought with sudden contentment, knit away and knit yourself back to sanity, and when you get back there, you'll find he'll be waiting for you, because the bitterness between you has no more than the venom of children in it....

She stood in her nightdress at her bedroom window an hour and a half later, the linoleum sending icy waves through her bare feet into every part of her body; but she didn't notice the cold for the iciness and loneliness inside her. The spines of rain splintered on the window panes began to depress her utterly. She turned from them and crept into bed. It was cold, and she huddled miserably, feeling that the whole world had become one great piece of ice.

She could not sleep, for a confusion of thoughts kept her brain in a turmoil. In spite of herself, she found that she wished she could speak with John. He was so level-headed and could make you feel that things were never as bad as you thought they were. Of course, she had fallen out with him, and he was feeling sore and bitter. Still...

But more than anything else, the thought of the lonely, beaten man in the little pink room twisted and coiled restlessly in her brain. She would doze for a few moments, only to awaken again, strangely frightened and very cold. Then, suddenly, a thought went through her like a needle of heat, burning her into complete alertness. She heard the voice in the shop again, quiet, infinitely sad answering the gloating question from Patch:

"I was condemned for jewel thieving."

Yes, that was it—I was *condemned*—not, I was *in for* jewel thieving. How could she have missed the significance of that answer. Excitement was like fire in her, and already she had slipped from the bed and was knotting her dressing gown about her. To go to a man's room at this hour was most unconventional, but she was in no humor for the conventions. She moved along the landing, flattening herself against the wall, because the center boards creaked. There were a few anxious moments on the stairs, when she stood with bated breath, waiting to hear her mother's: "Who's there?" Outside his door, she paused, quickly formulating the question that would force him to give the answer she knew he ought to give, and then stairs and landing could creak to their heart's content as she rushed back to raise the house—or the whole town, for that matter—to shout the truth about this man. And then, when she knocked softly on the door, she was amazed to find that it opened to her touch. She knocked again and it opened yet more. Cautiously, she looked around it, and stifled a little scream when she found the room empty.

She heard a steady drip, and because her nerves were so taut, she had a horrible moment in which she thought it was the dripping of blood. But she soon saw that it was water dripping from the flowers upset in a sodden heap on the window sill. And suddenly, as she watched them, she felt and knew something that was vague but very gripping. And she wanted John. She wanted him badly. She must get him, that they might find each other again in their search for this lonely and sorrow-marked man.

With the same great care, she made her way back to her room. Safely there, she dressed with feverish haste, throwing her clothes on her, buttoning her coat about her. Like a shadow she moved along the wall, down the stairs, and out of the front door. In spite of all her care, it banged, and the echo went in a soft rumbling thud to the ears of Mrs. McGough. Nell hastened away in the darkness to seek John. It was quite a distance to his house and every minute was precious. She began to run.

A window opened upstairs when she knocked at the door, and John looked out.

"Nell," he exclaimed in amazement. "I'll be right down."

She could hear his steps on the stairs, and a moment later he opened the door. A gust of wind and rain seemed to lift her and deposit her in the hall. His face still wore the look of amazement she had seen on it when he looked out.

"John," she gasped breathlessly, "please come and help me to find the Stranger. He has wandered off half demented with sorrow into the night."

She saw the expression on his face suddenly hardening.

"Perhaps the same gentleman has contributed a little toward making someone else—you used to know—half demented."

"But, John, haven't you heard about what happened tonight?"

"No," he answered, "I've been away till very late."

In a few stuttering words, she told him the essentials. He whistled softly.

"All right, Nell, I'll come," he said, and he turned and began to run up the stairs.

"Thanks, dear," she answered.

He stopped suddenly and twisted around.

"Thanks what?" he demanded.

"I said, *dear*," she answered, and he saw her stand for a second looking at him as she used to do, "and you'll find I meant it."

A second later, she was on the street again, rushing through the town. There was a song in his heart as he began to dress hurriedly to follow her. By a stroke of good luck, she chose to follow the Newry road as perhaps the most likely. She did not wait to question what she was doing or why she was doing so. She knew only an imperative need to act!

The echo that made a dull thud in the brain of Mrs. McGough brought that good lady quickly but cautiously to the landing. She called to her husband several times before receiving a sleepy grunt for a reply, followed by a disgruntled muttering:

"Well, has your friend Patch Rafferty discovered another jewel thief or what? Heavens above, haven't we had quite our fill for one blessed night!"

"Don't be so smart, Jimmy. I'm sure I heard the front door banging."

There was a shuffling and groaning of bed springs, and a moment later, he joined her. They moved quietly along the landing, and soon found that Nell's door was wide open. Mrs. McGough began to get a little hysterical when she discovered that Nell had gone.

"Oh, my God, what'll we do, what'll we do at all?"

"Do? Nothing!" he answered gruffly. "Wherever Nell is, she is all right. You have a chronic habit of forgetting that Nell is twenty-two years old, and not *two*!"

As though to emphasize this, the door of the little pink room suddenly banged.

"Heavens above, what's that?" she cried, her nerves beginning to fray.

"I'll soon find out," he answered.

A moment later, he returned and said:

"Looks as if you are going to be saved the trouble of turning the poor chap out on his ear, for he's gone himself. And Nell, bless her big heart, is gone either after him or with him."

"Jimmy McGough," she challenged indignantly, "you can stand there calmly while the whole world is going to bits about you."

"Feels solid enough to me, Mary," he parried, "and for heaven's sake, don't look at me with that self-righteous, Irish grocer expression on your face, which you wore so becomingly in the shop last night, when you assisted that scum Rafferty to victory by ordering Nell in like as if she was a little puppy."

She looked at him aghast.

"Well, I'm going to dress this minute and go after her."

"Oh no you're not," he answered. "I'm not going to let you make a public idiot of yourself and a laughing stock of me before the parish."

"You're the one to talk..."

"For God's sake, woman, keep to the point. Can't I just hear the sweet, simpering Mrs. Black enjoying herself immensely... 'Just fancy, my dear. Such a nice, sweet man he seemed, too, but then you never can tell, can you dear? And that good creature, Mrs. McGough, out in the pouring rain searching for him! So kind of her. But then, I suppose you couldn't expect a woman to live in the same house with such a sweet man without getting very fond of him. Don't you think so, my dear? I wonder what that good husband of hers thinks of it all...?'"

The landing echoed with his vicious, simpering parody of the good, kind, sweet lady, the sweet edge of whose tongue she had already experienced. She had calmed down considerably.

"I'll blow up the fire, then," she answered in a subdued voice, "and stay in the kitchen."

"Bring me up a cup of tea," he answered. "Seems it would be kind of soothing after all this."

He grunted with satisfaction that was partly relief at a crisis averted and partly self-congratulation at having so successfully asserted his authority in the house. Then he returned to his bed to await developments.

CHAPTER THE TENTH

Newry sits in a huge saucer of that rolling land between Dundalk and Belfast. It is fine rich land and it wears its beauty with a proud grace. But when rain sweeps into it, as it did on the fatal day of Patch Rafferty's disclosures, it can be as dreary a place as one would wish to avoid. Other towns just get wet; Newry goes one better by falling in with your mood and becoming as miserable and depressed as your dripping self.

It must have been putting forth a very special effort that night to match the wretched mood of a fat figure sheltering as much of itself as space permitted in the awning of a yard gate. The face was set in as stern lines as those loose globules of flesh would permit. The expression of the face was as dull and dead as the dripping wall that framed it. The head was drooped, giving a grotesque impression of a ball sinking in soft glue.

A girl was watching him from the other side of the street, where she stood flattened in a shop doorway. She drifted across the street to him, giving him a well-practiced flick of her eyes, the flying spark to kindle him. She saw that it went dead in the murk before it could light on him. But she was used to that. On nights like this, her victims were scarcely tinder.

"You're all wet, dearie. Like to come home?"

She stood in beside him, edging up to him tentatively. He had not turned to her, but continued to look straight into the murky darkness as though he was inhaling its mood, striving to merge himself and his misery with the night in a strange pantheism of misery and gloom.

"I have a nice room with a gas fire only a few minutes from here down by the docks," she went on. "Why not come?"

The last words were said in a weary voice that struck a note of kinship. They were two self-outcasts standing together in the night.

"Trade not so good?" he growled.

"No," she answered, edging nearer so that she touched him. "This place is too full of piety."

"Are you a Catholic?" he asked suddenly.

"Aye, of a sort. Used to be, anyhow. But don't let that worry you; you can't get soft on this job or you're done."

"Made your First Communion?"

"Aye, a long time ago. I had a white satin dress," she added with a forced laugh, "but there's a few spots on it since."

She was not playing her part with her usual adroitness, but she was too fed up to care. Her laugh was hard, bitter, cynical, the kind of laugh that has more of a death rattle than of mirth in it. He looked at her and she simpered at him, the moment of abjection having passed with the prospect of a conquest.

"Well?" she asked challengingly.

She was certainly attractive. Why shouldn't he? He was just sobering up a little after a heavy night's drinking. Why not, indeed? he asked himself as he looked at her again and let his mind kindle in the professional warmth of her glances.

"Come on, then!" he said.

She walked by his side. It was dark to the lamp at the top of the street. He put his arm around her and his fingers rested on the pocket of her coat. He suddenly felt as if he had been burned, for through the cloth he felt the shape of a crucifix. He drew his arm away quickly and stopped dead.

"What's up, dearie?" she asked in her professional simper.

"What's that in your pocket?" he asked.

"Oh, that," she laughed. "Them's beads."

"There's a cross on them—a crucifix," he said, and the word sent a strange coldness through him.

"It's a pair of rosary beads—my mother's," she said quickly, pulling them out and showing them to him.

They hung on her fingers in a tangle of disuse. The figure had been worn away on the crucifix by thousands of reverent kisses—her mother's kisses. The kisses of the daughter were for sale in the street. He stood fixed to the ground, his eyes riveted on the figure of the love-worn Christ; and through the film that a riot of thoughts was putting before his eyes, the hand that held the beads was age-yellowed, cracked, twisted with work—the hand of a mother that had prayed for him on just such beads as those. A mother had prayed for her, too, and he stood with this girl on the edge of the lamp's warm circle, with the knotted beads between them, as though in mockery of those prayers. Lust had gone cold in him, and he felt that the very slime of the street was rising to clothe him in a vesture worthy of the debauched state to which he had sunk.

She was looking at him in amazement.

"Feeling sick?" she asked. "Have some brandy—I always carry some with me."

He brushed aside the little flat bottle. She had put the beads back in her pocket, but he seemed to see them still.

"What do you carry that about for?" he asked thickly.

"Well, a sip on a night like this…"

"I mean the beads."

"Oh, the beads," she laughed. "Oh, it's just a habit. I can see," she went on, "that this little excursion of ours isn't going to come off, if you don't pull yourself together."

His hand was in his pocket, fingering the last of the pound notes he had received from his brother. Some more nestled in a thick wad against his chest. It had been an easy matter to push that seal-skinned, perfumed creature as she stepped from her car in a deserted street, snatch her bag, and make a getaway into a labyrinth of whose very existence the perfumed one did not even know. There was a bundle of about twelve pound notes, and a fence had given him thirty shillings for the bag. He stood with the girl, fingering the note. He drew it slowly from his pocket. Her eyes gleamed when she saw it.

"I could be doing with that," she said.

"It's part price of a coffin," he said slowly.

"Your own?" she asked.

"I wish to God it was," he answered with sudden weariness. "But it's yours without going another step," he added, drawing away from her and looking straight ahead as in a daze, "if you tell me whether a certain conjecture of mine is right."

"Well, ask," she said.

"You're hanging on to those beads because you're afraid to be without them. You have been trying to put a London Lisle Street layer of brass over yourself—to make yourself hard and chromium plated for your job. But you can't. The beads are the sign of your failure. The years of grace have left soft spots in you that won't harden. The grace of God is everywhere, and it splits its way even through brass."

"I don't know from Adam what you're talking about, for you seem to have gone delirious of a sudden."

She watched the note in his hand and began to bite her nails in vexation. Suddenly she turned to him, angry that such words should be wrung from her by a stranger, her face suffused with something that was like the struggling ghost of grace.

"The Mother of God never looked down her nose at the Magdalen," she said. "Does that answer you?"

"It does," he answered, holding out the pound.

She almost snatched it from him.

"I'd wash that Communion dress if I were you," he said quietly.

But she had turned from him. She hurried away toward the oily darkness of the docks. He noticed her drooped shoulders, all the sway and assurance gone.

"The Mother of God," he muttered, "never looked down her nose at the Magdalen." What a lovely phrase! he thought. It had a strange beauty, as if, in the gloom about him, he had suddenly met the odor of a rose. She was called a rose in the Litany. It was a long time since he had remembered that. Yes, that was it—Mystical Rose. The idea became a prayer: the first prayer that had softened the hard places in his soul for many years. And it had been put on his lips by a street woman. Such a grace was like a boomerang; it would probably return to the dejected, sodden girl who had been its pathetic instrument. Some morning, the Communion dress would be white again.

He could not see her now, but he could hear the hard tapping of her heels. They recalled the hollow sound of his own steps among the dripping trees in the night he had set off for Newry with Old Tom's money in his pocket. He had done many vicious and dastard things without turning a hair. Why couldn't he brush this matter of Old Tom's few pounds from his mind as easily as he had flicked the rest? After all, as far as his conscience was concerned, it was only a fly on a dung heap. Besides, it was Patch that took the money. How was he to know? But the fly grew on the dung heap, flapping itself, stirring up the stench of the whole. Luke Rafferty had reached the end of his tether.

Then there was this girl, coming to him when his depression was darkly pooled within him. For a moment, she had seemed a possible escape from his obsession. And then, he had suddenly seen this girl as an image of himself, as another of those tortured creatures who plunge themselves in the slime, and yet cling tenaciously to the hem of grace.

It is a pebble slipping that starts the avalanche. Old Tom's few pounds had begun it, and the rest—all once brushed aside cavalierly—emptied itself on him. But there was nothing dramatic or heroic about it, nothing of the majestic rumble of a landslide. It had as much dignity as the upturned contents of a thousand bins. His soul was cut and bleeding, but it was from the jagged edges of old rusty tins. There was nothing of heroic repentance—the dramatic call of a Rimbaud for the linen and the candles; the romantic cry of a Beardsley for the burning of his drawings. He just felt a fool, an empty fool forced at last to turn and look at his own hollowness, a dry fool standing in a drizzle of the ashes he had heaped in the hollowness of his triumphs.

It was a dangerous mood—the mood of proud self-disgust that made the halter of a Judas. He had wandered down to one of the deserted docks, and he stood there looking at the scum on the water. He saw that scum as his proper element: why not plunge into it and finish the whole business? There would be no tears shed when they fished the body from the tide—swollen, gross, revolting, like a Gadarene swine....

A white sea gull, as lovely as if formed from flung foam, swept bravely into the light where he stood, dipped to the water, skimmed it, rose into the darkness, leaving a spreading circle on the oily surface of the sea. It was one of those lone birds that, for some unknown reason, sometimes circle the dark docks and skim away. But its beauty was as a word of hope clearly spoken. He turned from the waters and began to walk into the town. Soon he found that he had taken the north road and was heading for the place from which he had so lately fled.

One idea had come to obsess him. He must return that money to Old Tom. He had accepted ten pounds of his money; he would return fifteen. Of course, they were fifteen stolen pounds, but he could do nothing about that now. Think of all that later. He must make "a start somewhere, and climb arduously back. Before he was halfway to the little town, he had made his plan. Old Tom's house was this side of the village. He would creep up to the door, and push the money in with a few words scribbled on a piece of paper. By standing in the road and holding the paper near to his eyes, he was able to print with some kind of legibility: YOUR COFFIN MONEY. He could not resist this touch of the macabre.

The headlights of a car coned the darkness behind him, and came to a standstill beside him.

"Can I lift you, Luke?" the voice called.

"Oh, thanks, Johnny. It's a welcome chance."

It was Fitzsimmons the grocer on his way from Dublin. He had been delayed by a puncture. Luke could not ask him to let him off at the corner of Old Tom's *bohereen*; it would be a strange place to choose. But where would he be getting off, anyhow? Unable to decide, he went the whole way to Fitzsimmon's bungalow, a few hundred yards north of the town. By pretending to be crossing a field to the other road so as to have a late drink in Martin's, he foiled any curiosity he might have occasioned. Doubling back, he began to return to the town.

To his left, standing back a little from the road, was the house of Father Seumas Sheridan. Luke paused by a gap in the hedge and looked in. The house was in darkness save for one lighted, uncurtained window in which he saw the priest was standing. Luke waited a few moments, but the figure in the window did not move. He walked on, opened the gate quickly, and went cautiously along the laurel hedge to where he could get a better view. The priest stood looking into the darkness, vaguely sorrowful, perhaps praying. There was a fine mellowness in the face, a soft kindness: the face of a man who had tears for all in sorrow and who knew the value of the smoking flax, the potential power in the bent reed. Luke felt drawn to him, and already he was moving toward the door. The priest seemed to have come back to reality with a start. He had drawn the curtains, but Luke could still see him silhouetted against the curtains. He knocked on the door.

Father Seumas stood in the opened door, holding a lamp in his hand. He raised it and looked at the man standing, with a strange suppressed excitement, on the doorstep.

"Oh, hello, Luke," he greeted him, "come along in."

Inside, the priest looked at him again, and saw the beaten look with which his years of ministry had made him all too familiar. The smoking flax, the bruised reed. He felt those great reserves of pity which he kept for all poor wretches, rising in him. For even when he goes to heaven, they will have to keep an eye on Father Seumas Sheridan, or he may attempt to get to Dives in spite of the chaos fixed between.

Always practical, he turned to his decanter and handed Luke a stiff whisky.

"You look as if you need that. Sit down, won't you?"

"Thanks, Father," he answered, and settled down in a chair to the left of the fire.

He could feel many of the carefully hardened places going soft in him, but he didn't care. He had surrendered to a man who met him with the sympathy of Christ. There had been no exclamation of amazement at a visit from one whose years, the priest knew only too well, had been a calculatedly cynical sneer at all that the Commandments stood for; no hard word had been spoken, no upbraiding look judged him, nor was there any hint of holy condescension toward an erring one—the kind of celestial smugness that sometimes spoils the manner of a priest. The eyes of the priest sitting opposite him were full of a fine, human sympathy for him. He knew that this man would lay down his life to save him from eternal death, and that the blood he would give would be rich, reeking, human blood, not a kind of angelic plasma. Luke knew all that, though the priest was merely sitting with him, quietly filling his pipe.

When Luke began to talk, it was as if the sluice gates of his soul had been opened. He talked as if to himself; he poured out, in a rushing stream, all those things that had gone sour in him and all the festering corruption of his years. Never for one moment did those eyes flinch; never for a second was the sympathy in them shadowed, not even when he told of the filthy way he had treated Father Michael Murray in that Brighton hotel many years ago. For Father Seumas had that wonderful power of concentrating on the poor swirl of human stupidity in the soul before him, and he did so now, with a strange feeling that all the power of his priesthood was rising in him to stem the wild excitement that filled him at this dramatic answer to his tormenting question. So the answer was yes! His intuition had been correct. This miller was a priest—a priest who had walked the wine press of his suffering until his feet were red with the blood of his pain.

But he must rigidly suppress these seething thoughts and concentrate on the soul before him. As he listened to him, the image that came to his mind was that of a mud-fouled river, carrying a wreckage of gold and silver that flashed in the sun. For there had been one crowded span of goodness, of striving for ideals, in this man's life that no amount of fouling could wholly foul. Many good men, troubled at no time in their lives with any thought beyond the reaches of their soul, and firmly moving in a rut of mediocrity, had less to show than this man.

When he had finished, the priest spoke to him as only a man like him could speak. With infinite tact, he approached the question of a written statement as part reparation to the wronged priest. Luke was most anxious to do so. For a few moments a pen scratched in the silence of the room, as Father Seumas bent over his desk. Twice he crumpled the sheets and threw them in the fire. Even in this, it was necessary that the man should feel the warmth of the Church toward him. Finally, he turned to him and read:

"I, Luke Rafferty, in the presence of the Very Reverend Seumas Sheridan, do hereby confess that on a certain night in the autumn of 19—, when drink had put me beyond the reach of the best things in me, I confessed to the Rev. Michael Murray—now known as "Miller" Michael Murray—in the Marisma Hotel, Brighton, for the sole purpose…"

He read it to the end. Every sentence was softened as far as possible, and there were no sharp, tactless edges on the words. It was a masterpiece of indictment, every word dictated by a glowing charity.

"…and as I hope for eternal salvation, I swear to the truth, the whole truth, and nothing but the truth, of everything I have set down here: so help me God. In testimony thereof, I hereto set my name."

When Luke had listened avidly to every sentence, warming in the charity of its phrasing, all the hardening of the years had gone. In a hand that shook with emotion, he signed the statement. The priest then witnessed it, and locked it carefully in his desk.

"You have done a fine and heroic thing, Luke, in owning up to that. It took a man to do it!"

Luke felt no stirrings of the heroic in him. He knew only that a great calm had settled on him.

"There is one thing more I must do, Father, I have told you of Old Tom's money and how I came to be involved in it. Well, it is by a mere accident that I called here tonight. Actually I came with the intention of making my way quietly to his house and leaving the money there."

"If you like, I'll give it to him for you, without your name, of course," the priest volunteered.

"No, Father, thank you all the same," he answered. "You see, I look on this as in some way a pilgrimage of reparation. And I want to make it now. Only, there is one snag. I stole this money from one of Newry's idle rich—I don't know from whom."

In spite of the situation, Father Sheridan chuckled.

"We'll discuss the *distinguo* and the *sed contra* of that some other time. Yes, perhaps you are right to finish the work you came to do, in spite of the fact that it is now two o'clock. But look here, Luke. You must promise to come back immediately. I have rugs here and you can doss down comfortably. Tomorrow, I hope for the terrific pleasure of hearing your confession and administering Holy Communion to you. It is one of the mighty moments in a man's priesthood when he is privileged to lift up a soul that has broken its wings bitterly in an effort to lift itself to the heights."

He would have liked to detain him to make his confession, but Luke seemed now very anxious to be on his way. Anyhow, it would be a matter of only half an hour or so until he returned, as he had promised to do. He watched him disappear through the gate.... What a wonderful thing it is that a man can roll himself in the slime, and then, with a word, a look even, rise to find himself clothed in the blinding whiteness of the wedding garment, with consecrated hands holding out to him—his God!

At the moment when the gate clanged to, the man whose innocence was proved in the document just signed, was wandering aimlessly, dazed, utterly crushed, in the fields behind McGough's; even while the priest was feeling the first great rush of joy in the thought that tomorrow, he would bring that mighty revelation to a man whose years had been shadowed. In the joy of that thought, Father Sheridan returned to his room.

A great crucifix hung in the room with a *prie-dieu* before it. He knelt, that he might pray for all earth's tangled things that find their only unraveling here. Weariness came on him, for it had been a heavy and exacting day, and he was suffering the reaction from the emotional strain to which he had just been subjected. His head fell heavily on his arms and he was soon asleep.

A huge marble clock stood on the mantelpiece. It was one of the kind that seems to be ticking its way solidly, stoically to eternity. It ticked its way through the half hour... through the hour...through many hours in which Luke Rafferty did not return.

CHAPTER THE ELEVENTH

Luke Rafferty made his way through the deserted street. It was dark and the only life there was in the flickering of the gas lamps, the crazy drizzling of soft, insidious rain into which the storm had abated, and the sudden streak of a dripping cat from one side of the street to the other. The gaslight flickered on its oily body as it crouched, sprang, and merged with the darkness. There was no need for cautious movement yet, and his heavy footsteps were hopping balls of hollow sound among the houses. Here and there a curtain was drawn and sleepless eyes looked out at him, glad of anything to break the dragging monotony of the night hours. At the end of the street the light of a police torch suddenly ribboned the darkness, rested for a second on him, then faded with a satisfied click. To increase that impression of all being well even in the dreariest of dreary nights, he called out:

"Bad night this," in a voice that had the bell-like conviction of a good conscience in it.

"Rotten!" came a growled reply. And then for good measure: "Filthy!"

When he got on the main road beyond the street, he began to walk cautiously, keeping well into the shadow of the hedge, where the soft ground deadened the sound of his feet. He slipped precariously once and cursed fervently. Then he grinned ironically in the darkness; it was natural to expect, he thought, that his first act of grace after such a long period of disuse should creak at the hinges a little with a curse or two. He stood when he reached the corner where the *bohereen* joined the road. A rough stone wall made a kind of dam there, and the recent rain had stirred the stagnancy of the pool that filled the dip. The neck of a half-sunk bottle showed darkly at the edge.

He listened carefully, but except for the querulous sound of the wind through the high grass, he could hear nothing. He could not hear an alert footstep moving quietly around the back of the house at the top of the hillock.

Old Tom had made up some of his loss. The miller had given him a couple of pounds, and others had followed his example. It was something to begin again with; and it brought new courage to the old man. The near edge of an open grave was coming closer and closer to his feet, for at his age the years sloped downhill rapidly; but he would cheat it yet, and there would be no pauper's sod to mock his independence and his pride. Sometimes, in the quiet of the night, his delirious old brain would see a great river of red grave soil moving toward him. He would then seize his new bank notes, wave them in the air, curse and pray in one breath, and fill the attic rafters with crazy, quivering laughter as he saw the soil recede, his vision clearing. The miller had advised him to leave his money in the post office; he had even arranged with the postmistress to show it to him, still safe and sound, every day. But no, he would have none of that. He knew another place where he could hide it. Aye, it would be safe with him. They left it at that, and none of them noticed something ominously grim in the way he had said it would be safe. Old Tom had always been such an eccentric that they failed to see that he was now mad and filled with the strange cunning of the mad.

He was guarding his money with a long, vicious carving knife which he spent an hour sharpening every day. He had also a family formula for a certain rat poison, which had been improved by several generations until it reached its final perfection as a very demon of poisons, through a new ingredient added by Old Tom himself. Rats had been found near it, as stiff as if carved in wood. One little drop of that in a man's blood....

He had chuckled the morning the idea came to him. He had chuckled as he sharpened his knife. He had continued to chuckle as he reached for a certain bottle on a high shelf, took it down, holding it carefully well away from him, poured its thick green contents into an old tin, and dipped the knife deeply into it. When he lifted it, let the drops fall carefully off, and held it to the light, it gleamed with the ghastly greenness in the pallor of a corpse.

He had taken to sleeping during the day, that he might be able to mount guard over his treasure at night. Around and around the house he prowled, the green blade gleaming damp in his hand. Each round ended with a visit to the house to dip the blade again, that it might be always wet and always ready.

Luke had begun to creep cautiously along the hedge. He had taken the fifteen notes and folded them with his written message, so that they could easily be shoved under the door, and he held them ready in his hand. So intent was he on his stealthy advance, that he did not see the figure crouched, in the ditch, eyes insanely fixed on him, corpse-green knife quiveringly raised. He crept nearer the door; only another ten yards or so and his pilgrimage was complete. A demoniacal scream made him swirl around, but not in time to dodge the vicious knife thrust of the old man. He felt the maddening pain as the wet green blade sank into his flesh and remained there. The old man sprang back from him, and began to laugh hideously. Luke gripped the knife and pulled it out, pain racking every-nerve in his body as he did so. He still had energy enough to leap forward and plunge the knife into the idiot shaking with insane laughter at the rush of blood that had followed the knife. Luke stepped forward, snarling, the knife raised. Then, suddenly, he stopped, controlled himself with all his will, and, turning, flung the knife into the hedge. In that moment, Luke Rafferty had prayed. It was more than a mere determination not to kill, and more than a mere discarding of a knife, it was an act that gathered Luke Rafferty's soiled years into one moment that he might disown them. In that moment, Luke Rafferty rose from soul slime and stood arrayed in the whiteness of the wedding garment. Its price was the price of blood—his own, oozing, poisoned blood, suddenly lifted up in atonement for his years.

Old Tom had fled, but his chuckling filled the lane until he reached the door and banged it behind him. He had not noticed the blood-stained money lying on the ground, with its grotesque legend: YOUR COFFIN MONEY.

Luke turned and began to drag himself toward the main road. Every movement was agony, and sometimes the pain took a paralyzing grip on him, so that he had to steady himself against the hedge. He struggled to the road, but the poison had begun to work in real earnest and the loss of blood had made him extremely weak. He collapsed on the grass edging, his head toward the stagnant water.

The Stranger had plunged blindly into the darkness, thirsty for the solitude and the nameless peace it offered to all the seething things within him. The darkness was friendly, the sodden earth kind under his feet. He wandered aimlessly through the fields, the fever subsiding in him as the cold and the wet seeped into his bones. In its place came the dull emptiness of those first few hours in the prison cell. For the first time in all the years of his trial, he had lost grip and he knew a strange bitterness of soul that bade him to throw the priesthood from him—to give back to his God a gift that had made a mockery of him. Coldness was through him, like ice in his veins. And why? Because it must not be known that he was one of God's Anointed. Of God's Anointed? Rather, one of those chosen to be lifted to the heights—and then flung down like a thing accursed!

The ground was suddenly hard under his feet. He shook himself out of his daze and looked about him. He did not know how long he had been wandering, or how long he had lain in a hopeless huddle when he had collapsed once in the soggy grass. To his amazement, he found himself on the Newry road just a little outside the village. He must have turned, somehow, in the darkness, and come back on his tracks. One light, only, made a little window high up in the dark. He recognized it as marking the house of Old Tom—another of life's derelicts with whom, at this moment, he felt a dull, dreary kinship. Wearily, he set off toward Newry. His footsteps echoed among the trees with a dull, sodden sound.

At the corner of the lane, a deeper patch of darkness suddenly stirred and groaned. Delirium had set in, and a mad mosaic of the fragments of his years, passing through his mind, was the soul's answer to the poisons in Luke's blood. He was again in jail—one of a sullen row of men walking across a prison quadrangle, every face heavy and bitter... "Who is he?" "Don't know; caught with the rocks." The haunting eyes: the light, the peace, the pain in them—the eyes of Christ when, turning, he looked upon Peter. It had once been a horrible silence of beaten men, a silence full of eyes, of eyes that had the soul-searching cleanness of the dawn in them. With the awful silence of death closing in on him, Luke thought that he saw the eyes again, but they were dead and empty eyes like the eyes of a corpse.

And then, for a moment, the film of delirium and poison cleared from his brain, and he saw those eyes, now suddenly become eager and alive, looking at him. He thought it was just part of the chaos and wild illusions of a poisoned death. But the eyes remained, and suddenly hands were on him—strong hands, hands as gentle as the hands of a woman—raising him, and a soft voice asked urgently:

"Are you all right, Luke? Can you hear me, Luke?" And then, in sudden alarm, a heart cry: "Good God, you're bleeding!"

Luke could not speak. There was a torrent of words rushing through his brain, but he could not speak. God, if he could only speak! To tell this priest how he had suffered for his treachery to him. To let him know that a document had been written and sealed. Above all, to tell him how the moral victory shining in peace through the pain in those eyes had haunted him, giving him no rest. How he could see those eyes now brimming with sympathy for him, and how they looked like the eyes of Christ greeting him at the grave. Luke did not know that his own eyes had become eloquent, too, words crowding from them that this man had a strange power to read.

One hand was under his head, the other raised in absolution over him, and the words were a wave of peace passing through his tortured mind and body. The words came clearly to him, for they were spoken loudly with a strange, burning enthusiasm into the silence of the night:

"*Ego te absolvo a peccatis tuis in nomine Patris et Filii et Spiritus Sancti....*"

The words were so fervently spoken that they seemed to fling a burning cross on the air above the dying man. Fascinated, he watched it. It came nearer, getting smaller and smaller.... And suddenly it was the little crucifix in the hand of the street girl, but he knew it was not the street girl, he knew it was the hand of the Magdalen. And then that crucifix seemed to plunge into him, to rack every nerve of his body, to run through his marrow like liquid pain; and the confusion of hell, a mad medley of howling, seemed to accompany it all. Then suddenly a bell tolled, deep and soft in its note and curiously like the voice of the man still bending over him. The voice and the bell began to merge, and the merging became a prayer spoken in words that had the great softness of summer rain in them. In their strength, in the comforting peace they brought to him, he found strength to raise himself and speak a few words. They came in low, gasping whispers, but the head bent to his heard them all.

"It's nearly over...Christ...is...a gentleman.... He does such thoughtful things.... I want you to know..."

The head sank heavily on his breast, and the sympathy-brimmed eyes gazing into his became the eyes of Christ. The oblation of blood in the drab lane, with the stench of the stagnant waters for its incense, had risen to heaven as an acceptable sacrifice, and the fire of final purification had been its answer.

A tremendous sense of exaltation, like the rush of blood to an atrophied limb, had come to the Stranger. All the weary despair of that empty wandering in boggy fields had left him.

In its place had returned that other moment when Mauriac's words—"mercifully hurled against the wood…"—had been flung in letters of sound on the air, and splintered to fill his cell with the voices of hope. Those voices were about him now, in a darkness that no longer promised a defeatist peace, and in the large drops of rain that had again begun to fall. He had gone on his knees beside the dying man. His head had become heavy on his supporting arm. Gently, with the gentleness of a woman, he removed his arm, that the head might rest on the grassy part of the ground. When he rose from his knees, everything began to swirl about him. The exaltation of again administering a Sacrament had been too much for his exhausted state; his legs went weak under him and he pitched forward in a dead faint on the grass beside the huddled corpse.

In a second, a girl was beside him, her face chalk white with fear, her black hair thickened with the rain, her hands trembling. She had flung herself on her knees and was bending over him, chafing his hands and face that were stone cold to her touch.

"Michael, Michael!" she whispered hysterically. Then— "Oh, my God, what am I saying! Father, Father!"

Quickly she removed her coat, and folded it under his head, the lining outward. The rain swept her, quickly soaking the flimsy cotton frock she had thrown hastily on, and sticking to her like a second, clammy skin. She had run through the darkness from John's house, and at the corner of the lane she had seen the curious tableau of two figures. She stopped and then quietly approached. Then the quiet air had been filled with a deep, strangely triumphant voice, and she had sensed, rather than recognized, that the "miller" was giving absolution. Good God, a priest! She thought suddenly of that kiss she had given him in the mill and horror rooted her there. Then he had stood, and she had seen him pitch forward on the grass....

She turned and began to run toward the street. She had not gone far, when John arrived, pushing his bicycle with all his might against a head wind. He thought his sight was playing him tricks when he saw her coming running through the driving rain, her dress clinging to her, her hair like thick wet ropes clung in confusion. Utterly amazed, he dismounted beside her. They stood together for the first time since their bitter parting, and in spite of the cold and the driving rain, in spite of her soaked and bedraggled appearance, the beauty of her wildly excited face went through him like a knife. He threw his bicycle on the road, stripped off his coat, and put it about her. His hands lingered on her shoulders. Impulsively she clung to him, lifting her face to his. He kissed her, his arms tightly clasping her to him, and she felt all his lonely hunger in that kiss. Then, quickly, incoherently, she told him what had happened. She told him the "miller" was a priest, but even in her excitement her good sense did not desert her, for she warned him not to say anything.

"It is his own awful secret, John. We must keep it."

In a matter of minutes they had a car to the spot. Luke was obviously dead, but the Stranger was breathing. Quickly they lifted him into the car. Nell, being slight and taking up little room, got into the back with him. She supported him, his head heavily limp on her arm.

"I hear he's an ex-jailbird, and that Patch Rafferty found that out," the driver remarked to John.

"Maybe there's a thing or two more that long bony lath of an idiot didn't find out about him," John answered grimly.

"What would that be, now?"

"I'm not saying."

Mrs. McGough opened the door and stood firmly in it.

"So my traipsing nightwalker of a daughter has come home, has she? Who have you there? If it's that fellow…"

"The man is dying, maybe. Have a bit of sense, Mother."

"Oh, it's like that, is it? My own daughter…!"

"I wouldn't own you for a mother if you turned a sick man from your door," Nell answered, flying into a temper such as her mother never saw in a child of hers. "If he goes, I go, for I wouldn't cross your door to share the curse of Christ that will come on you!"

The mother backed from her in amazement. Nell directed them with their burden into the kitchen. Some brandy revived him a little, and the two men carried him to his room. They undressed him, dried him with hot towels, and put him to bed. John had called back something about hot-water bottles to Nell. Her mother was dumbly helping her to prepare them. It was not that Mrs. McGough had none of the milk of human kindness; she had not slept, she had discovered that both the Stranger and her daughter had left the house. It has been a relief to see Nell at the door, but the reaction had set in immediately and she had taken up quite another attitude. Besides, some of the broken glass which had escaped the brush squeaked under her feet as she went to open the door, and served to remind her of the unfavorable turn her business might take as a result of the night's doings.

They scarcely had him settled when Nell came up with three hot-water bottles. With infinite care and a respect he could not conceal, John arranged the bottles about the sick man. Nell went down again for her knitting—knitting is soothing to upset nerves—that she might sit with him till her messenger returned with the priest. But there seemed little need now, and she began to regret having sent, for the warmth had revived him and he had dropped into an exhausted sleep.

The owner of the car returned to it. Several people had come out on the street, for you can gather an audience easily enough when excitement has made the neighbors "sleep all the night with open eyes," like Chaucer's birds. As he came down the stairs, he wondered what on earth John Boyd's reverential attitude could mean. When he suggested bundling him into the bed quickly and unceremoniously— why, Boyd had almost panicked! And what could he have meant by that snappy remark about Patch? Surely, if any man should rejoice in another's disaster, John Boyd should rejoice in this man's. And yet, the careful arranging of the hot-water bottles, the smoothing of the sheets, the puffing of the pillows…?

The door of the car had been left open, and a book lay on the running board. He picked it up, opened it and turned to the people. At that moment a woman emerged from the next house to McGough's, and said:

"I seen that dropping from his pocket when you were lifting him out."

She peered at the book and gave a little scream:

"My God, he's a priest. I have a brother a priest and I know. He's a priest, all right."

A card slipped from the book where it had marked the Office of the day. It commemorated the raising to the priesthood of Michael John Murray.... Six frightened eyes read it together. A sudden hush came on them and into that hush the town clock let four tired notes fall. Yet, in spite of the lateness of the hour, the news had begun to spread.

It reached Big Bob Mullins, when a handful of gravel thrown by Tub Regan splayed his window and he raised it to see what was wrong. Ten minutes later, he had joined Tub and they were quietly knocking up three or four others. And half an hour later, a cattle truck pulled out from a yard, with six grim men crouched in it. It drove a little along the North road, and pulled in on the grass a little way from a hovel that stood on the roadside.

There was no light in the window. They crept up silently, two taking their places by one window, two by the other, and Regan by the door. The sixth remained with the truck. Regan knocked. There was no reply. He knocked again. Still no reply. Impatience got the better of him and he kicked the door. A chain rattled inside, and a moment later a window was pushed up.

"Who the hell…?"

"Hell yourself!" came the quick answer, as two huge hands gripped his throat and heaved. Patch found himself dragged through the window, bound, gagged, and lying on the ground before he quite knew what had happened to him.

On the way they told him that they were about to show him what happened to people who called a priest a jailbird. They were taking him, Regan snarled in his face, to see a horse doctor about the mad accusation he had made against the Reverend Father Michael Murray. Patch started when he heard this. He saw Luke's face again as he had seen it in the booth—absurd with surprise, blanched with fear, the mouth hanging open, on a cushion of chins. And he knew now why this had been. He could not answer the men, for they had gagged him; he could not tell them of the horrible, cold fear in the pit of his stomach, that was not fear of them. He lay grotesquely absurd on the floor of the truck, his dirty white nightshirt torn at the neck, his bony legs sticking out of it, matted with red hair.

"You look a fair sight of a man, this minute, Detective Rafferty," Regan jeered. "There was a dance on in Clogoghue last night. Pity we hadn't you in time for it. In that getup, you'd be the belle of any ball."

They pulled into a quiet side road very near Newry. A bucket of tar, two big whitewash brushes, and a bag of feathers were deposited on the roadside. They lifted Patch out and propped him against a wall. Then, coolly and casually as though it were just a job of work, they tore the shirt from him and tarred him thoroughly. Regan, with, great gusto, sprinkled the feathers. They reminded him that a barracks was near at hand where they might help him to join the white race again. Regan told him he should take to the air. But no monkeyshining though—they warned him—or the police might be interested in knowing who stole Old Tom's money. It was a lucky shot in the dark, for they had never got past the stage of a shrewd guess.

The truck had been backed into the road, and the engine was throbbing. They cut the cord that bound his arms. The knot holding his legs was easily opened, and they left him to it. A minute later, the truck had passed out of sight over the brow of the hill.

Patch struggled out of his fetters and made for the road. He was walking fast and the heat of his body was already beginning to make the tar grip and burn him. A horse shied at sight of him, and the owner cursed it to a standstill. He had been going to collect his load for the Newry market, but he altered his plan. He turned the cart, asked Patch to climb in and lie on the straw, and silently handed him a sack. It was dressed in this that Patch arrived at the police station. He was attended to there, and, when questioned, said he had no charge to make. A tarring is a rare occurrence and the victim generally has asked pretty often for it; besides, the name Patch Rafferty was not unknown to the police, so there was no fuss. Patch never reappeared in the town. There is a rumor that he joined the British army and deserted later.

Meantime, Boyd had arranged for the removal of Luke's body. The man who had been sent for Father Sheridan had returned with a strange message. He faltered over it, like a man who still cannot believe he has heard aright.

"The priest says—says—God's truth, them's his very words—that you're to bring the body of Luke to the priest's house and call Mrs. Mulvaney."

(Mrs. Mulvaney was an old lady whose chief joy in life was the washing of corpses. Her sympathy was not complete unless, to the phrase—"Ah, it is poor Johnny Reilly, God rest his soul?"—she could add—"Ah, sure, it was myself laid him out!") The news that the priest had sent for the remains dumfounded them all. It amazed John Boyd, who returned to the spot, stood looking down at the body. It was a rather repulsive-looking sight, huddled there in the mud. In fact, it was just as Luke himself had pictured it—gross, swollen, like a Gadarene swine flung up on the beach after its careening fall to death.

But when they turned him, so that his face showed fully in the gray of the false dawn, they were awed by the peace they saw on it. It gave them an inkling of why, maybe, the priest had sent for them.

"Them priests do have strange knowledge," someone remarked to Boyd when they had settled the body. "A priest can know as much as God Almighty Himself, sometimes, about what goes on inside a man."

"Aye, surely," another agreed. "Sure, isn't their confession boxes the wash of the whole world's waste."

"Luke was a rum one, God rest his soul," remarked the third, who was still gazing at his face, "but there was always something you couldn't help liking in him, and he looks as if he finished well. He hadn't a hundred sharp and cutting corners like Patch has. Wishing the man no harm," he went on, "but I'm thinking it's himself should be lying there."

Instinctively, they looked up at the little house crowning the hillock, but as they drove away no one made any further remark.

Father Seumas had been stunned by the news. He returned to the room, and as he did so, a newspaper cutting, with heavy headlines, caught his eye. It had been blown under his bookshelves and had remained there unnoticed until now. It was the account of the case of a certain Michael Murray, priest of the Roman Church, condemned for theft. He had been vaguely dissatisfied with it all at the time and he had kept the cutting.

He rejoiced, as he pulled on his coat hastily, that he had now the answer to it locked in his desk.

CHAPTER THE TWELFTH

He had abandoned himself to utter exhaustion, Nell thought, like a tired swimmer who suddenly gives up the struggle and sinks into the deep water. In sleep the lines of his face had softened and the impression of a guarded secret they had always given her was gone; he suddenly looked very young. Not for one moment had she left the bedside, and once, when he had turned in sleep and flung his arm on the counterpane beside her, she went on her knees and kissed it reverently. Not like that had she kissed him in the dim interior of the mill, for then it had been the anxious, fearful gesture of a girl whose love had suddenly broken bounds; for now, it was a gesture of all the intense reverence in her pure soul toward the priesthood in this man whose gentle sorrow had made her love him. She was not ashamed of that love. She was only ashamed that he should know of it. At the slightest sign of wakening, she would rise quickly, step back into the shadow made by the corner alcove, and stand quietly there, ready to slip from the room. She had done this hastily, when the tired arm had been suddenly flung on the counterpane beside her, and only when it had lain quietly there for a few moments had she dared to creep forward and imprint on the consecrated fingers her reverential kiss. He must not find her there; he must not know whose hand moistened his fever-parched lips, tending him with all a woman's lovely solicitude.

The flowers she had arranged so carefully the evening before lay in the huddled, sodden heap into which they had fallen when, eagerly pressing forward to the coolness of the panes, he had upset them. That they lay so crushed and broken did not distress her, for, with that strange intuitive wisdom of a woman, she had her fingers on the pulse of those fast fevered moments in the room before he plunged into the darkness. Her intense sympathy figured the face again for her, pressed to the glass, eyes thirsty for darkness. She entered into his agonized moment, and she saw those sodden flowers as the symbol of the inadequacy of earth's love to soothe the exalted agony of a soul whose sorrow had no craving for the earthly in it. Earth's greatest gift to a man is the love of a good woman. She had offered that gift to him, raising her hands high in the offering that she might reach the exalted heights of him. But she had been standing in the plain, and his feet had rested on the mountains far above her, where the air is not softly tender with the loveliness of women, but radiant with the whiteness of God and quiet with the exaltation of His prayer.... Her flowers of offering had dropped from her lifted hands, her eyes dazzled by the naked light that had seared her, when she saw the hand she had kissed, just now, raised in absolution amid the murk and the mud. These flowers of earthly comfort, offered in love, might now, indeed, be an unlovely heap at her feet, but they were wet with human tears of which she was not ashamed, and scattered in a moment of blinding reverence—a moment in which, it seemed to her, the curtain of rain and mud had been parted that she might see the priesthood, blindingly, in a raised hand. And she knew this as a mighty grace not given to many.

She would later guess that three blinding graces had met in the murk of that corner; or rather, that grace had visited the gloom, and that three souls—the soul of the priest, the soul of the dying man, and her own—had been as mirrors held up to it, flashing that grace one to another, after God's fashion of making human souls the instruments of His gifts. In the clairvoyance of death, with eternity in the air about him and sympathy-filled eyes on him in soothing caress, Luke Rafferty had known that wonder. He had seen it as the gentleness of Christ.... "Christ is a gentleman," he had said with a magnificent audacity of expression, in an effort to give human words to a blinding moment of grace. For he had seen the face bent over him, the hand raised in absolution, as a mighty personal gesture of Christ when the darkness about him was thickening to the darkness of death. But it was not that which had summoned all his strength to utter those strange last words; it was rather the sudden flooding of the dead, despairing eyes of the priest, at the moment when the thrill of administering the Sacrament in reality to the

169

man who had received it from him before in mockery and with a Judas kiss, had given new life to the hand lifted in absolution and to the beaten soul lifted suddenly in prayer. Gross, sodden, ugly he might well be; yet he could still be the merciful instrument of grace in the hand of Christ toward the man he had cynically ruined. The bruised reed could still show lovely, raising itself from the slime; the smoking flax could still give the flame, long struggling and now blazing forth on the edge of the grave.

All this Nell would guess at, when she had pieced together into one design the fragments of her experience and the words she would hear from the priest himself. Now, she knew only that she had been caught up in a moment of tremendous experience as a vital part of that moment; and that in it, the years of her girlhood had ended and she had deepened into maturity. The girl who had turned to John Boyd, face uplifted to his kiss, dress clinging like a second skin, was a girl who had come of age in a blinding moment. It was from this new and frightening maturity, also, that her mother had quailed.

A step sounded on the landing, moving quietly. She had been lost in thought, and therefore it was with a frightened expression that she saw Father Sheridan entering the room. He greeted her softly and went to the bed. His fingers were gently on the sleeping man's wrist, testing his pulse, but he was not too absorbed to notice that Nell was edging toward the door.

"Don't go, Nell," he said quietly. "I want to see you."

He put his hand lightly on the forehead and found it cool. Then he turned to the girl.

"He'll be all right, Nell. Sleep is nature's finest medicine."

She suddenly began to cry, all the pent-up things welling in her. He stepped forward and put his arms about her shoulders.

"Don't, Nell, don't. What's the matter, child?"

His soothing voice steadied her a little, and she looked up at him, the tears streaming from her eyes:

"Father, he'll be all right. Yes. He'll waken up, but to what, Father? To the priesthood that he must keep hidden in him like a dark, horrible secret. They say he was in jail. I don't care, I don't care!" she went on frantically, the words all the more gripping for being whispered. "I know he's good and kind and—and—like Christ!"

It had been a great rush of words, and Father Seumas was looking at her in amazement.

"How do you know he is a priest?" he said.

Brokenly, incoherently, she told him her story. With some difficulty he pieced it all together, and through it all he caught the glimpse of the spiritual experience it must have been for this girl.

He held her out from him, and looked into her tear-filled eyes.

"You loved him, Nell?" he asked quietly.

She lowered her eyes in confusion, but she answered bravely.

"Yes, Father, I loved him. But now I know that it wasn't any kind of love like mine he wanted, but something grander and higher. I don't feel like that, anymore, and"—she went on, looking with magnificent candor at the priest—"I'm not ashamed of it. Maybe the little kindnesses I showed to him helped him a little in the hard way he was going, even though his sorrow was too great and too holy a sorrow to lose itself in the softness of a woman's love."

"I'm glad you're not ashamed, Nell," he answered softly, "and I'm sure he saw the gentleness of Christ in you. And when he wakes, Nell, it's not to sorrow and secrecy he'll awake, but to this!"

He drew Luke's statement from his pocket and handed it to her. She trembled as she looked at it, and the silence of the room seemed to deepen about her as she read. It might be the priestly, suffering silence of the sleeping man now terminated by the document in her hand.

Her face radiant with joy, she turned to Father Seumas. He would say, afterward, that he never saw a more beautiful expression on a human face.

"I knew it, Father, I knew it! And I knew he was a good man even at the moment when everything was black against him."

She handed the paper back to the priest, and they stood together, watching the sleeping man. There was a throbbing joy in the silence, and its center was the pure and generous heart of a girl.

"I am proud to think," Father Seumas whispered, "that my parish is so blessed with a girl of such charity and vision."

For two days she nursed the sick man back to strength, and with a gesture worthy of the fine things in her, she renewed the flowers in the room. Then the moment came when Father Seumas thought fit to show the document to his fellow priest. Nell had left her patient asleep, and was downstairs washing potatoes, just as on the day the Stranger arrived. She was thinking of this and of the heaped-up things that had filled the few weeks since then, as she listened to the footstep coming into the shop. She was drying her hands to go out, when the kitchen door opened, and, to her surprise, Father Seumas walked in. He usually came by the hall door, not through the shop and pub.

"I knew I would find you alone," he said, greeting her, "and that was how I wanted it just now. I have a special and very pleasant favor to ask of you."

"Yes, Father?" she answered, surprised.

He drew the document she knew so well from his pocket and handed it to her.

"We'll go up to his room, together, now, and you will present him with this," he said.

"But, Father…" she said, suddenly confused.

"No 'buts,' Nell. There were no 'buts' in the girl who told me a few nights ago that she was not ashamed!" he countered.

She laughed softly.

"Father," she said, "you are very kind to make me the chief actor in the happy end of a drama into which I was so strangely caught up. It has all made such a change in me. I seem to have lost the selfishness that was in me. Yes, Father, I'll look back on this as the greatest thrill of my life, and I'll remember that it was your kindness that made it possible for me."

They went up to the little pink room together and found him sleeping.

"I'm glad he is sleeping, so that you can awaken him to this," the priest said to her. "It will be like raising him from the deep valley of crucified silence, to where light and comfort awaits him."

She approached the bed timidly and laid her hand on his to rouse him. He awoke to find his faithful nurse beside him, her eyes filled with a strange light.

"Father Michael," she said, her emotion and the relief of at last using his title giving to her voice a splendid ring. "I have something for you. Read this."

She held it open before him. He read for a moment, bewildered, thinking that his dreams had begun to mock him. But the paper that met his eager, outstretched hands was real; the tears of joy in the lovely eyes were real, too. He sat up slowly, reading it, its message seeming to pass into him like a current of new life. Weak with reaction and relief, he sank back on the pillows, murmuring:

"Thank you! Thank you! God is good to me."

It was at this moment that Father Sheridan stepped forward and handed him an open telegram. The sick man held it before his eyes, reading it in a kind of daze.

Father Michael Murray. Complete restoration to all sacerdotal functions and privileges. Congratulations on magnificent steadfastness and courage through years of darkness. God bless you.

✠ John, Bishop of Exmund

Father Seumas had lost no time in forwarding all information to Father Murray's bishop. Even before the dramatic call to his bedside, the letter, with a copy of the confession enclosed, lay on his desk ready for posting. The promptitude of the reply witnessed to the immense joy with which the news had been received.

"Father Seumas," the patient said, "this is very typical of the kindness which saturates your priesthood and every action of your ministry. Though I may have been so assiduous in avoiding you," he continued with a smile, "that did not prevent my noticing many things. Don't think for one moment that I was unaware of you in your lonely visit to that country church. No, Father, I wasn't, for the air about me seemed suddenly warm with your charity and your prayer for me. But I could not speak, because of the great, silent secret buried in me, and its visible evidence in the breviary I clutched quickly from your sight like as if I had been discovered in a secret sin. That was the hardest thing of all, Father, to have to shun those who are my brothers in the priesthood of Christ. But all that's over now. God rest the soul of poor Luke! There were great things in him, but they got tortured and twisted."

175

"Lie quiet now, my son," Father Seumas said, his voice soft with tears. "It's all over now. The altar is before you, my son, manna-white with the Host that awaits your consecrating touch. With what tremendous depths of new realization will you say those opening words of the Mass—*Introibo ad altare Dei*—'I shall go unto the altar of God'?"

"Yes, that is it," the patient answered, with a smile that lighted up his face with great beauty. "*Introibo ad altare Dei....* A new realization!"

He seemed suddenly lost in thought. Father Seumas raised his hand in blessing over, him, and tiptoed from the room.

Ten minutes later, Nell, ever vigilant for her charge, returned quietly. He appeared to be sleeping. She left a glass of water on the little table beside him, and had almost reached the door, when he called her softly.

"Nell, please come here for a moment."

She returned and stood beside him. His eyes remained closed, and for a long half minute, he did not speak. Then he said:

"Nell, you left the room while the priest and I spoke together, and so you didn't hear me tell him how all the time I appeared to be avoiding him, I felt the warmth of his priesthood and his prayer about me."

He paused. Nell wondered why he had said this to her.

"Yes," she said, twisting self-consciously the engagement ring which John had put on her finger only the day before. "He is a grand priest."

"But I felt another warmth in this new crisis of my sorrow, Nell," he continued, opening his eyes and looking at her with a soft, grave depth in them that was lovely to see. "I felt the warmth of a woman's kindness—of your kindness, Nell. Don't be ashamed of it, Nell—especially, don't be ashamed of your little kindness and overflow of lovely, womanly emotion in the mill. I could do no more than give a hint to you then, and I worried later lest any word I said might have had a hard edge on it. Sometimes, to encourage myself, I used to imagine that I was walking my silent years step for step with the silent walk of Christ to the mount of His crucifixion. I like to think that it was at a moment of tremendous spiritual desolation for Him, that a woman called Veronica stepped forward and wiped His face with a towel and that His divine will permitted that this should be a mighty, human strengthening for Him on His way.... My years, Nell, were a way of loneliness and sometimes there were moments of hollow discouragement when I felt I could endure it all no longer. That moment in the mill was one of the blackest of these, and in it you came to me and your kindness was the towel that wiped my face. You spoke to me—you told me I was good and pure and kind; you did not know it, Nell, but every word of that was a hand reaching into the darkness of my soul, gripping me, drawing me toward the light of hope. I asked you to remember those words at another time. You did—you remembered them magnificently when every hand seemed turned against me, and I became a fallen idol to these good people. In a way, Nell, you have had your reward—the reward of being caught up vitally in a moment of intensity, when grace flashed blindingly from soul to soul by an act of what Luke, in a magnificent dying word, called the gentlemanliness of Christ. But I shall also make a gesture of gratitude to you, Nell, when I breathe your name over the consecrated Species in the first act of my restored priesthood."

Tears streamed from her eyes as she listened to him. She threw herself on her knees beside the bed and, in a voice choked with emotion, she asked him to give her his blessing. Slowly, deliberately, with all the solemnity of a priest's first blessing on the morning of his ordination, he blessed her. Then, as is customary, he offered her his hands that she might kiss his consecrated fingers. The kiss which she imprinted there with such intense reverence, seemed suddenly to overwhelm, swallow up, and exalt the kiss given in the mill, so that she saw it as something pure, and not the least shadow of shame could remain.

She rose quickly and left the room. Anxious to be alone, she slipped silently down the stairs to the first landing, and closed her door quietly behind her. She threw herself on her bed and buried her face in the pillow, that she might have a good cry.

The news went through the town like the leap of terror through a crowded street. The reaction was a dumfounded silence, broken only here and there by sudden outbreaks of accusation and counter-accusation among those who had been prominent in the mob moment of a few nights before.

There was a spinning and a counter-spinning of rumor that webbed the talk of street and hearth and pub. Then, on Sunday morning, Father Seumas spoke a few words, and they were like fingers pulled through that web, scattering it with the shock of a wonder at which the wildest weaver had never guessed.

He had finished the announcements, laid the book aside, and he was standing for a few seconds in silence. Expectation had been running high; you knew that by the absence of the chorus of sneezes, wheezes, coughs, and general nasal and larynx trumpetings and scrapings that usually accompany the items for the coming week, and swell to a grand overture of shuffling feet, general rearrangements, fine trumpetings and wheezings given out with grand abandon on every note of the scale, just before the sermon. For the people knew all the signs: the mistake or two in the announcements, due to his brain being "a bit scattered by other things," and, now, those few seconds silently watching his hands as though something was written on them. Not since the Sunday after the disgraceful conduct at the Lurgan match, some months ago, when tempers had boiled over, was there such a grave-side silence in the church.

He did not say much, and they knew that every word had been thoroughly weighed beforehand. He told them how Tobias, in the Old Testament story, had entertained an angel unawares, and how it had been given to this parish of theirs to do something like that. "Miller" Murray, he went on, is the Reverend Father Michael Murray of the diocese of Exmund, a silent martyr through dark years of imprisonment because the seal of confession commanded him to silence when he stood convicted of theft. That was all over for him now, and soon they would have an opportunity of praying for and with him. Meantime, the priest went on with quiet emphasis, let there be no further acts of stupidity. He paused for a moment and then, in a tone that indicated an apparently complete change of subject, he asked for prayers for the soul of Luke Rafferty whose remains had been interred in the local cemetery on Friday. He began an "Our Father" and turned to the altar, sending the prayer in a curving ripple over the heads of the people. It returned to him in a low, rumbling wave that filled the sanctuary about, him, full of sneezes, wheezes, coughs by which a churchful of people register a sudden relaxing of unnatural tension.

There had been a twelve-month ration of excitement and tension in the past few days. There had been Patch's crowded hour of glorious life with—to quote Regan's venomous witticism—its tarred and feathery sunset; there had been the news of Luke's murder, and the wonder of the remains being brought to the presbytery; there had been the excitement centered around the news of a priest living secretly among them, with all the tangled skein of rumor that went with it; and finally there had been the macabre scene at the inquest on Luke. Old Tom had been in hiding, and the closest search did not find him. He burst into the inquest on Saturday, however, his white hair flung, his eyes insanely bright, and, standing there, he had laughed and laughed, bending and slapping his knee. They surrounded him, gripped him, and forced him to a chair. In the scuffle, a wad of bloodstained notes fell from his hand, and were scattered on the floor. There was a piece of paper, also with something printed in pencil on it, but it was too blood soaked to decipher.... Father Seumas knew that the reaction from all this was in the shuffling, wheezy, prayerful wave surging about him....

At McGough's, Nell had taken command of the situation in a firm manner. She allowed no visitors to the sick priest, but she took messages, fruit, and delicacies for him. Finally, these came so frequently that she had to refuse them. Under her vigilant care, he made a quick recovery, and after a short convalescence during which he remained quietly in the house or puttered about in the big garden, the doctor brought him the good news he had been thirsting for—the news that he was now strong enough to say Mass. It was a Sunday afternoon, and at the devotions that night, Father Seumas announced that the Reverend Michael Murray would say Mass at half past nine the following morning. The news spread through the town and countryside.

From early next morning, they began to gather, and soon the town was as packed as for a fair day. But they gathered quietly, and even with a certain solemnity. Carts lined the streets, and cars of every description—from ancient Fords, with an air of having strayed from some mechanical Limbo, to their streamlined, vulgarly opulent descendants—rattled or snub-nosed their way into the town. By the time Father

181

Murray was ready to leave his little pink room, a great crowd had gathered at the church and along the road leading to it. Father Sheridan had a car at the door to take him to where he would know again the ecstasy of offering God to God.

His progress there was as slow as a triumphal march. The crowd, caught up in the excitement, had pressed about the car, and the driver had the sense to yield and make the car, as it were, walk with them. The crowd in front and behind continued to increase, making a human stream on which the car seemed to float. The noise of voices filled the air like the murmur of mammoth flies, until it was drowned in a thunder of clapping hands, as the surging crowd saw the man they had known and loved as "McCourt's Miller," stepping from the car in the black clothes of the priesthood.

Tommy Muldoon, the new miller, served the Mass. He had had quite a job brushing up his Latin for the occasion. Things like *quare tristis incedo, dum* and *quoniam adhuc confitebor* are hard to get out trippingly at the best of times, and much more so when there is a lump in your throat and your eyelids have to keep blinking rapidly to stem back the tears.

The crowd filled the church, the porch, the doorway, the churchyard, and there were even some who had to remain on the road. Yet, for all that, the silence was deep and awe-filled, becoming profound and gripping as the bell rippled its silvery message, that the hands which had so often helped to load their carts were now about to command the presence of their God among them.

They were calloused hands, especially by contrast with the white purity of the Host he held. That rough skin might serve as symbol for those years of pain, that, in this moment of surging happiness, he might lift them up in the sight of angels and of men.

"*Hoc est enim Corpus Meum....*"

The little bell seemed to catch the words and sprinkle them in silver drops on the uplifted, tearful faces of the kneeling people.

Made in United States
North Haven, CT
09 February 2025

65186869R00108